P9-CKA-224

Perchance to Dream

Colleen Mariah Rae

Perchance to Dream

Colleen
Mariah
Rae

HAVEN HILL HOUSE

All rights reserved under International and Pan-American Copyright Conventions
Published by Haven Hill House, P.O. Box 8018, Santa Fe, NM 87504
© 1992 by Colleen Mariah Rae. All rights reserved
Printed in the United States of America

This is a work of fiction. Names, characters, places, and incidents are either the products of the author's imagination or are used fictitiously. Any resemblance to events or persons, living or dead, is entirely coincidental.

No part of this book may be reproduced or transmitted in any form or by any means, electronic or mechanical, including photocopying, recording, or by any information storage or retrieval system, without written permission from the publisher. For information address Haven Hill House, P.O. Box 8018, Santa Fe, NM 87504.

Publisher's - Cataloging In Publication
(*Prepared by Quality Books Inc.*)

Rae, Colleen Mariah.
    Perchance to dream / Colleen Mariah Rae.
    p. cm.
    ISBN 1-880382-00-8

    1. Reincarnation--Fiction. I. Title.
PS647.W6   813
                                              QB191-1482

Cover Photograph © 1992 by Steven E. Counsell
Book Design by Haven Hill House

For Dylan

To die, to sleep—
No more—and by a sleep to say we end
The heartache and the thousand natural shocks
That flesh is heir to. 'Tis a consummation
Devoutly to be wished. To die, to sleep;
To sleep, perchance to dream. Ay, there's the rub,
For in that sleep of death what dreams may come,
When we have shuffled off this mortal coil,
Must give us pause.

Hamlet (Act III: Scene I)

"Bergie, for God's sake! What is this? Listen to this. Are you there, Bergie? The headline in the *Minneapolis Star* reads, 'Woman Found Levitating in SW Desert, Body Smells Like Roses.' My God, Bergie! Is that you? Bergie, come home. You're too old to be doing things like this. What will your grandkids say?"

Bergen rubbed her thumb over the tip of the pastel crayon she held in her hand. "Settle down, Kristian. You're acting like an old man."

"I am an old man. Seventy-five, Bergie! Too old to be reading stories about my wife levitating in a desert. Doesn't do the old ticker any good, I'll tell you. Bergie—are you there? I'm coming down."

"No."

"I'm coming to get you."

"Why doesn't it say 'artist found levitating'?"

"Don't try to change the point."

"No. Why? Why 'woman'?"

"It says here, Bergie. In the story. 'Once-famous artist Bergen Klein.'"

"Once famous!"

"What do you want at seventy-two?"

1

"Artist at least! After sixty years, don't you think it's earned?"

"Nuts! That's what you've earned, Bergie. Nuts. A handful of very loose marbles."

"You talk to the counter for awhile, Kristian. I've got work to do." Bergen laid the receiver in the crumbs next to the toaster, filled her mug from the coffeepot, and sat down at the kitchen table. She could hear Kristian's voice buzzing on.

"Gnats, gnats, gnats. The whole world's filled with gnats," she said as she added burnt umber to the mindscape she was drawing.

Coyotes barked and God opened the back door. He saw Bergen sitting at the table, and walked in with his brown, chipped mug in his hand. He poured himself a cup of coffee, pointed it at the phone, and said, "Your phone's off the hook."

Bergen tapped the table, and God sat, his dreadlocks swinging like jungle vines with his movement. He stared at her over half moons of black he'd painted under his eyes. The odor from his dungarees filled the small kitchen. "What you drawing?" he asked.

"My conversation with my husband."

"The one what's talking to the cupboards?"

"The only one." Bergen pushed her thumb hard against the umber and smoothed it slick over the undercoat of dusty pink. "Want to draw?"

"Naw," he said. "I got no art. That's why they keep locking me up, I guess." He tapped the empty space in his smile. "Vietnam, you know."

"Wasn't there," said Bergen. She scratched at the pastel with her fingertip, cross-hatching. "World War II. That's where I met him." She nodded toward the receiver. "Parachuting in. Behind enemy lines. Never marry a Norwegian." She rolled her eyes and said loudly. "Berserk, you know."

"Come home," shouted Kristian over the phone line. Bergen nodded at the receiver. "Coming to get you," he shouted, and then the phone went dead.

"Do you think he's really coming here?" asked God as he watched the dial tone oscillate from the receiver.

"I don't know, but I'm going to paint," said Bergen. She pushed herself back slowly from the table, floated through the sine waves, and hung up the phone.

It was mid-afternoon before the phone rang again. Bergen didn't hear it. She was lost in the water swirling around the dolphins. She couldn't get the color right. Nothing ever looked as good as the colors she saw in her mind. Her dream colors were even more vivid. She squeezed some cerulean on the waxed paper palette and pushed the edge of her fist into the blob. Solti's baton spun the passages of Beethoven's Pastoral against the canvas, and she met the resonance with the heel of her palm, spinning her fist upward like an unfurling underwater plant. The swath of deep blue moved upward with the dolphin, with the music.

"Why do you always paint dolphins?" asked a voice

from her feet.

Bergen looked down at the sand eddying across the bare planks of her studio floor. She heard snuffling and turned toward the bay window, her blue palm raised, her eyes swimming to the surface.

"Why dolphins?" asked God. He'd raised one of the windows from outside, and he and three of his coyotes stretched their heads inside.

"How long have you been there?" asked Bergen as she wiped her hand on a rag.

"Long enough to know you're not answering the phone."

"Did it ring?"

"Where you been?" asked God.

"Painting," said Bergen.

The coyotes whined at the window. "It's a girl this time," God said. "You should answer your phone. It's not your husband. It's a girl who used to know you. Someone you parachuted with. She's calling right now," he said as the phone rang.

"Hello," said Bergen into the receiver.

A young woman's voice asked, "Is this the famous artist, Bergen Klein?"

"See, I told you!" said God, his eyes spinning out like Ezekiel's wheels.

Bergen waved her hand at him to be quiet. He climbed in through the window and squatted, pulling his bony knees to his emaciated chest.

"This is Bergen Klein, yes."

"Finally!" said the girl. "I saw the article in the morning paper, and I couldn't believe it. Bergen Klein! I've been looking for you for years!"

God tugged his knees closer to his chest and nodded gleefully. Bergen turned her back on him and the coyotes that were crawling through the window.

"For years!" said the girl.

"Katherine," whispered God. "Her name's Katherine."

"Katherine?" asked Bergen.

"I knew you'd know me!" squealed Katherine. Bergen held the phone away from her ear and watched the looped notes bouncing off the floor. God tapped the planks until the notes lined up and skitted over the sand to his finger.

"Where are you calling from, Katherine?"

"She's in town," said God.

"I'm at the Safeway. Around the corner. I was wondering if we might meet. For lunch. Oh, it's four already, isn't it? For dinner. Could we meet for dinner?"

"For dinner?" asked Bergen as she studied her paint-creased palm.

"Oh! I know it's an imposition," said Katherine. "But I've waited so long and looked so hard. I'm just so excited. Tomorrow? Or the next day? I don't mean to impose."

"No, dinner is fine. Do you know the burrito man? Ask at the Safeway. I'll meet you there at five." Bergen set the receiver back in its cradle. "Five," she said to God. "We'll meet her there at five."

"No," he said, tucking his knees under his chin. "This is between you and her. You'll see."

Bergen combed her short white hair, arched her still-black eyebrows with a spit-wet thumb, and smoothed her skirt over her protruding hip bones. She slipped her big broad feet into blue baby dolls. It was a long walk to the burrito man's.

Her shoes said, "We could fly."

"You never know who you're going to meet," said Bergen as she buffed the top of her shoes with a lambskin puff. "If you don't mind too much, we'll walk."

The blue shoes danced her feet. "Saxophones, that'd help."

"Flamenco," said Bergen as she flipped on her portable music maker. The Romeros carried Bergen and her shoes out the door, down the dusty streets, and to the path between the phone company and a crumbling adobe wall. There her feet caught in the ruts, and her ankle twisted. "Owwh!" said her shoes. "Enough with the flamenco, already."

Bergen floated into a small courtyard surrounded by adobes and filled with giant oaks. She settled next to a y-shaped stick that propped a wire clothesline strung with flapping diapers. In the very middle of the courtyard on the old henge stone, a girl sat dropping cornhusks onto a bed of coals.

"Katherine?" The name feathered the black curls at the base of the girl's neck.

She turned like a whirligig toward Bergen. "You're here," she said, bouncing up from the stone. "Bergen Klein!" She bounded toward Bergen and hugged her tightly to her round bosom. "Finally! You're here."

Bergen pulled herself free. "Haven't you got it confused? Isn't it you who is here, Katherine?"

"You haven't changed one bit," said Katherine as she clapped her fat hands together. "I love it! Not one little bit. How long's it been? Well over forty years, and, by God, Bergen, you're still the same!"

Bergen leaned close and stared into Katherine's blue-black eyes. In them she saw the flagpole on the roof of Notre Dame, two young women climbing it. Climbing high above Nostradamus, the gargoyles. High above the Seine, the old city below. Wearing striped cloth shirts and apache scarves tight at their necks. "Katherine?" said Bergen with awe. "How can it be you? You're twenty if you're a day."

"New body," said Katherine as she did a pirouette. "I was tired of war-thin, and they gave me a choice when I was reincarnating, see. 'Ectomorph, endomorph, or mesomorph. Check one, and only one.' That was easy." She patted her arm that was a big as Bergen's waist. "Sumo. That's what I'm aiming for. Then next time I fall, I'll bounce!"

Bergen's shoes started singing: "Falling, falling, falling down. Falling, falling down."

"I haven't heard that one," said Katherine.

"Oh, it's a tune they picked up somewhere. You don't remember falling, do you?"

"C'mon," said Katherine picking Bergen up by her waist and walking with her toward a screen door that hung by one hinge. "First, let's eat. I'm starved!"

The door flew open when they got to it, and Bergen's shoes shrieked. The burrito man stood with his crooked back to the door, flipping tortillas on the black surface of the wood-burning stove, chortling.

"Why do you always have to scare my shoes!" shouted Bergen.

The burrito man laid his nose on his shoulder and skewed his eyes at Katherine. "*Chica*," he purred. "What you doing with this *vieja verde*?"

Katherine hoisted her body up to his counter and crossed her legs seductively. "*Vieja verde*? That's a good one coming from a dirty old man like you," she purred back.

"*Dos burritos, El Malo*," said Bergen.

"She's always calling me names," said the burrito man, stroking Katherine's cheek with a greasy, tangled finger.

"That's maybe because you never told me your name," said Bergen.

"I don't give my name to *brujas* like you. But to this one! She can have what she wants." He tried to slip his arm around Katherine's waist, but it was too broad for

8

him to reach.

"Burritos," said Katherine. "Two for my friend here; five for me." She slipped down off the counter.

"One's all I want," said Bergen.

The burrito man rubbed his thumb and index finger together. Bergen waved her hand and a dollar appeared. "I don't want none of your air money," he said.

"All I got," she said.

He looked at Katherine. She shook her head. "*Dos burritos*," he said. "*Es todo*." He slapped tortillas on waxed paper squares; dumped a stew of meat, potatoes, and green chile in the middle of both; and rolled one with each hand.

"You come back," he said to Katherine as he handed her the burritos.

"*A bientôt, mon cheri*," cried Katherine, Bergen, and her shoes as they fell tumbling like rolly-pollys out the door. They laughed all the way to the plaza.

"I see you still have your touch with men," said Katherine as she studied the white letters on a red and blue sign. "'Do not move the banches.' 'Banches'? They don't mean these, do they?" She hoisted a bench and moved it into the sun. The old men hunched over chessboards "tsked" in unison. Katherine and Bergen laughed, and sank onto the bench, and unwrapped their burritos, and both took bites.

"I can't believe you're really here!" said Bergen with her mouth full. "How have I lived forty years without you?"

They sat quiet for a time, chewing on the burritos,

letting the green chile trot down their nerve endings and ping in their brains like pinball machines on tilt.

A whistle dipped from a dead branch above their heads. Bergen threw a bit of tortilla up, and a mockingbird caught it midair, held it between its wings, and floated down to the bench. "One one thousand. Two one thousand," it chanted, holding the tortilla to its breast.

"Do you know this bird?" asked Katherine.

"You should know him, too. Remember Frederick? He died the same day as you." Bergen took a bite of her burrito, and her breath steamed.

"Frederick! Your lover?"

"Don't tell Kristian."

"Who's Kristian?"

"The man I married. I met him the day you and Frederick died."

"Ah, yeah," said Katherine. "That guy in the barn. He was a Norwegian, wasn't he?"

"I *thought* you were around that day," said Bergen. Frederick had hopped onto her finger. "I just couldn't believe you were dead. Both you and Frederick impaled by those trees. It was a ghastly sight, believe me. I tried to get you down."

"I know."

"Why'd they only send three of us to do that job?"

Some of God's coyotes were skirting the plaza. Bergen whistled, and they sped pellmell toward the sign, jumped it, and settled at her feet. Frederick jumped on the head of the biggest.

"They were pals, too," said Bergen. "I don't know any of these guys from before, but I guess Frederick was a Navajo for a while before this." She leaned down toward his sharp beak. "What I can't figure is why he decided to come back as a bird."

"I didn't have that choice," said Katherine. "Mine was 'male, female, hermaphrodite.'"

"What'd you pick?" asked Bergen.

Katherine punched her on the arm. "Still a joker. Haven't changed at all, have you?"

"A bit. I kind of got trapped in this old body."

"I don't remember ever being old. I guess I must have one time or another, but I just don't recall it. Is it bad?"

Bergen held her hand out on her lap. "I can't believe it's my hand. I look in the mirror, and, after thirty years of wrinkles, I still am surprised at the face looking back at me. I can jump rope in my head, but my knees creak when I walk. It's tough being stuck in a body."

"Maybe you're about ready to let it go."

"I'm working on it." Bergen crinkled the waxed paper into a ball, tossed it in the air, and blew it toward the waste bin. It arched and dropped straight in.

"Brava!" said Katherine, Frederick, and the coyotes. The old men on the benches just "tsked."

"C'mon," said Bergen. "Let's go home!"

The night swallowed them, dark as their anger. Frederick double-clutched the Model B, downshifted as the hill dropped. His tight-clenched hand couldn't stop the *brrr* of the loose stick.

Bergen sat straight in her seat. "I'm not going to Spain," she thought. "Not! Not! Not!"

The car lights made thin circles on the road. They were alone in the black night, black as Frederick's hair, black as her own.

"My hair wasn't black," said Bergen.

"Yes, it was," said Frederick. "Black as your eyebrows."

"No! My hair was always lighter than my eyebrows. Much lighter."

"Well, I remember it black."

"You would, bird brain."

"What's that supposed to mean?"

"Do you see colors?" asked Bergen.

"Now you mean?"

"Yeah, now, in your life as a bird?"

"Well, no."

"So, of course that's all you remember. My hair wasn't

black. And besides, there was a moon that night. It was 1937, there was a full moon, and we were on our way back from that dance in Albuquerque."

Bergen remembered the feel of the heavy black crepe dress wrapping around her thighs as she and Frederick did the Lindy on the crowded floor. It was in the car, on the way back, that he'd told her he was joining the Lincoln Brigade and wanted her to come too.

"I am not going to Spain," she said. "And if you loved me, you wouldn't be going either." The engine roared in the silence like her anger. She shoved her shoulder against the bare glass, wishing she could push right through, roll out onto the road, into a ditch.

Frederick reached up to adjust the rearview mirror, and his silver ring flashed the moonlight into her eyes, drew her eyes to the rivulets running from the square turquoise stone, to his hand, long and pale in the moonlight. She watched his hand adjust the mirror, and his hand stirred her need to feel him again, deep inside of her. The thought built into a memory strong as reality, and her body flushed. Then it faded. "No," she thought. "I will not go!"

The car bounced disturbingly down the dark road, Mozart on the radio.

"We didn't have a radio," said Frederick.

"What do you mean?"

"There was no radio in that old car."

"I remember one."

"There wasn't one, I tell you."

"I remember music!"

"Sure. I was singing!"

Frederick was humming "I'm an Old Cowhand (From the Rio Grande)." She looked at him for the first time since she'd told him emphatically that under no condition would she go. Not to Spain. No. She looked at his mouth ready to break into song and almost laughed, but his eyes were focused far away. She seized her hurt around her like a baby's hand tight on a finger.

The dark rolled by, mile after mile. Frederick was humming "Summertime" when she saw the road to San Felipe pueblo ahead. She looked at him again, his arms encircling the steering wheel, his wrists crossed and each finger curled from behind, fitted into a wedge on the wheel. She reached out and touched his fingertips. The shock was like flicking a switch on a generator. Her body started to pulse and she wondered if it were coursing through him, too. He took her hand, looking at her surprised, sad still. She saw the sign. "San Felipe." "Want to get off and find a big rock to park behind?" He looked at her, and then downshifted. She put her hand on his thigh, where it belonged. The truck rolled down the ramp to the stop sign. He sat and turned to her, questions in his eyes. The traffic rushed white streaks over the bridge above to their left.

"Wait a minute, Bergen! There was no highway then. No off-ramp!"

"Oh, you're right!"

Around them the silent pueblo night circled. He

14

turned right and drove the car down a rutted dirt road, past two spots where other roads, side roads, were bitten through the creosote-held dust. The car dipped down to into a sandy flat spot, and Frederick said, "Here?"

"No!" she said with a laugh. "Not in an arroyo. Can't you see the headlines! Lovers found floating upside down in a Model B! They'd love that in Santa Fe."

Frederick steered the car up the other side. A short distance farther, a road cut to the right, curving like a snake path toward clumped mounds of earth rising in the moonlight.

"Here?" he asked.

"There's even a rock."

Frederick turned the car onto the cross-rutted path and aimed for the stand of rocks. Beneath the outcropping circled a flat spot. He pulled the car into its talcum-soft surface, driving over the crunch of creosote under tire, and turned the ignition off.

"Come over here," he said.

She shook her head and motioned to him with her index finger. He laughed and tried to shift over to her seat, but his long legs stuck in the wheel well.

"Tsk, tsk," said Bergen. "You'll have to walk around."

"You're a cruel woman!" he said as he opened his door. The night slipped in and curled around her.

"Oh! Close the door. It's cold!"

Frederick slipped his legs, then his backside out, but leaned toward her, across his seat, trying to kiss her.

She pushed him away. "It's as cold as you."

15

"We'll see about that!" He slipped out, closed the door, and, with a quick run, vaulted over the hood of the car.

Bergen pushed the lock down.

Frederick pressed his face tight to the glass and mouthed the words, "Let me in."

She shook her head.

He smeared his lips over the glass in a huge, "Please."

Bergen wrinkled her nose and shook her head slowly.

Frederick stood up and dug into the pocket of his gabardine slacks. He pulled out a silver dollar and pressed it to the glass.

"Nope!" said Bergen.

He dug deeper and came up with a $20 gold piece.

"Double nope!"

He squatted next to the car, his chin on his fists, watching her through the glass. His eyes lit up. He stood, slowly unbuttoned his fly.

Bergen's tongue touched the tip of her teeth.

"Ahh," he said and stuck his hand into his fly.

She opened the door and turned so he could slide into the passenger seat. Then she raised her full skirt and straddled his legs. He played his hands under her black dress, up along her bare legs, over the silk of her drawers, back out again. With both hands, he cupped her breasts and buried his lips against the crepe, licking round and hard over her nipples, sucking hard. She moved forward, rolling her pelvis toward him.

"You'll come with me?" Frederick asked as he unbuttoned her dress and pulled her breasts free.

She ran her hands over his chest. His nipples were hard under the cloth, under her hands. "No," she said, and kissed him.

His left hand slid under the skirt of her dress, up under the edge of silk, and his fingers found their way to her crotch and tucked inside and nestled like a warm burrowing animal, bumping gentle and soft against her clitoris until the wanting grew and she broke away from his hand, slipped into the other seat, and raised her bare feet to the cold windshield in front of him. She leaned back and lifted her hips and eased the silk slowly over her legs. His hands followed.

"You too," she said and helped him unbuckle his belt and his trousers and slide them over his upraised hips, over his knees. And his penis curved large and firm above his belly. And he moved toward where she lay across the other seat, his penis falling ready toward her and her eyes got big and wide and she said, "Over there. I want to get on top." And he nodded and they flowed together back to the other seat and she pulled her labia wide and cupped his penis head.

"Will you come?" he asked.

"No," she said, and licked her fingers and moistened the side of her vulva and slid down him, taking him tipping inside of her, his penis pressing, curving, arching to encircle her womb and stroke it and round it. And they moved. She rose up and settled, rose again and drew him in, deeper and faster. His hands rolled her hips closer toward him, the crepe caressed her leg with each movement, his body rose with hers, faster and faster. And her orgasm built and built and she felt a cry deep in her throat and felt the black curling from her toes up like hot milked waves into her head that closed like a door on a kiva, closed to contain the pulse from the earth's core. The dark light. And it grew and grew and grew and her cry got louder and the pitch of their movement deeper. And she cried out and he cried out and they came together like drum thunder over rounded walls, like fire rising up a chimney with snow cooled heat. Together they came and kept coming clasped tight in and around and over and under and through each other like a mesh of sinew and nerve interweaving into one God sigh. Ahh. And the tension went. Their bodies collapsed into separateness and the skin of her breasts still tingled and she nuzzled deep into his neck to smell his smell, to lick his skin, to burrow there forever.

They sat like that for a long time, silent. His skin grew cool wet, and she opened the window. The air rolled over them with the bite of green and dew-filled mornings in its breath, of winter being seized by spring.

After a long time, he said, "We better go." He opened the car door, slid out, and bent to pull his trousers up. The moon melted like mercury over his behind. "You have such a cute little ass," she said.

"*Moi?*" he said.

She slipped her black pumps on her feet and stepped out of the car into the soft dust. "I need a lava bush," she said.

"Will a tire do?"

"Don't be rude," she said as she walked around the car. "And don't watch."

She squatted, her skirt hitched up, her feet sinking into the ground. She watched her water spread like a dark lake on the soft talcum earth. She wiped herself with a makeup cotton ball, buried it and the puddle with her feet, pushing soft white powder over the dark circle.

When she stood, he was behind her, slipping his arms around her waist. She spun around and looked up at him and his head was circled with a halo.

"It wasn't!" said Frederick.

"It was the moon!" said Bergen. "The moon had that big, wide ice-crystal circle around it, remember?"

"No."

"It did."

"You said you'd come with me then."

"I didn't."

"Yes, you did."

"I never said I'd come with you. Not then. But I knew. I knew then I'd come with you. To Paris at least."

"You'll come then?" asked Frederick as he started the Model B's engine.

Bergen leaned her head on his shoulder.

"You won't be sorry," he said.

Bergen watched the parachutes falling down from sky.

"Yes" is all she said.

Katherine slipped a bare foot out from under the comforter. The studio floor sent the hot shock of ice through her bones. She drew her foot back in, pulling the down puff close around her head, trapping the smells from the kitchen in a warm pocket of air around her nose.

"Green chile!" she thought and threw back the covers and landed with both feet bouncing across the icy floor to a pair of oversized lamb's wool slippers.

As Katherine walked out the door, a furious ball of black made one swift rabbit leap, grabbed her ankle, encircling her sleep-warm skin, teeth fighting bone, back paws a staccato beat. "Ahhh!" shrieked Katherine, shaking the battling fur into a jar of brushes, rattling them over the cold wood floor.

"Grandma!" shouted Bergen from the doorway. "I'm sorry, Katherine. I should have warned you." She picked up the cat by the scruff and stared into its eyes that were yellow as her own. "I don't care what body you're trapped in. You do not have to play the part. Besides, it was your doing, if you remember. Your choice, if I recall?"

The cat tucked its hind legs up tight to its body and snarled, "Put me down!"

"If you promise to behave."

"Put me down, I said, and I won't tell you again, Bergen."

Bergen settled the cat on her shoulders and sat on the bed next to Katherine who was examining the puncture wounds in her ankle. "Look what you did, Grandma," said Bergen.

"It'll heal," said the cat, stretching luxuriously on Bergen's bent back.

"But, Grandma, what if you have rabies?"

The cat pulled itself erect on Bergen's left shoulder and said, "If I have rabies, Bergen, isn't it your fault?"

"Grandma, hunh?" asked Katherine. "I heard a lot about you. Warm, cuddly, loving."

"She was all that," said Bergen.

"What do you mean 'was'?" said the cat, jumping down from Bergen's shoulder and arching its back under Katherine's hand.

Smoke curled into the room with little cloud faces puffing the warning: "Breakfast, burning, burning, breakfast."

The three of them tore into the kitchen. Bergen grabbed the salt and doused the flames.

"How *can* you burn eggs, Bergen?" asked the cat as it batted the smoke with a paw. "I don't understand it. I taught you to cook. Look, they're black."

Katherine and Bergen looked at each other and their laughter burst like seltzer in water. "Eggs!" gasped Katherine.

21

"*Les oeufs, mais oui, mamselles!*" shouted Bergen through her snorts.

"*Mais, garçon? Ils sont un peu noir, n'est pas?*"

"*Ah, non. Ils sont parfaits.*"

Katherine looked into the pan. "*Ah, oui, parfaits!*"

"What are you two talking about?" asked the cat. "Can't you speak English? Or German? Or Norwegian even? You know I don't speak French."

"*De rien,*" said Katherine, and they both peeled with laughter, their skin falling to the floor into jiggly heaps.

"Horrible!" yowled the cat. "Pull yourselves together!"

Bergen and Katherine laughed until the windows shook and God stuck his head in the door. "What a mess," he said.

"Taste this," said the cat, hooking a glob of black egg on a claw.

God sucked the egg through the hole in his teeth. "Too much salt. By the way," he said to Bergen, "your husband called."

Bergen composed herself. "When?"

"When you were meeting Katherine. I didn't answer the phone, of course, but it was clear his intentions."

"He's coming?"

"Yep," said God.

"Your husband's coming here?" asked the cat, clapping its paws in glee.

"But you never liked Kristian."

"Oh! Is it that one? I thought it was Frederick."

"Grandma, Frederick died more than forty years ago.

You know that."

"I lose track of time."

"Excuse me," said Bergen. "I'm going to call him. I'll use the phone in my studio."

"Never saw what she saw in that guy," said the cat. "Not as bad as her father, mind you. No, that man Cally should never have married. Did you know Cally?"

"Didn't she have red hair?" asked God.

The cat nodded.

"A dancer? In New York? Died of cancer, didn't she?"

"It was because of that man. She should never have married that man! But she was like me," said the cat.

"Never could tell her nothing," said God.

"Just like Bergen," said Katherine. She melted some butter in a clean frying pan. "Eggs all around?"

"No, make mine over easy," said God.

"As long as they're not burned," said the cat, "they're fine with me."

Bergen came back in the room and slid into a chair by the stove. "He wasn't home."

"He will be soon," said God.

"Breakfast is served," said Katherine as she set four egg-filled plates on the table.

"Do you like stories?" the cat asked Katherine between mouthfuls.

"Watch out for her," said Bergen. "She's a Siren."

"Then I'm safe," said Katherine. "Protected by my gender."

"Oh, no," said God. "That was the generic 'men,' you

23

know. Homer wasn't sexist. Not at all."

"Whatever you say," said the cat. "You're the one should know."

"Now, don't fight!" said Bergen, pushing her plate away and pulling the cat into her lap. "When I was little, Grandma was always telling me stories."

"It was the only way I could get you to come out from under that big old table."

"I liked those claw feet."

"I'd pull you out and sit you on my lap, and you'd still be patting the table."

"I remember. That wood was so soft."

"You liked to have worn it out—that and the spot in the lino you were always circling with your hands and your cars."

"That dip! It was like a crater, and you'd always set the bread to raise right in that spot, in that big old washbasin, square on top of that spot."

"The sun was there."

"Grandma, Grandma, Grandma!" said Bergen scratching behind the cat's ears.

"A little lower," said the cat. "Ah, that's good."

Katherine gathered the empty plates and put them in the sink. "I bet I know what Bergen's favorite story was," she said.

"Bet you don't," said Bergen.

"I'll bet you a two-dollar bill!"

"You're on."

"It started, 'The sun rose pink,'" said Katherine.

"Ha! You lose," said Bergen. "She started all her stories like that. In her world, the sun was always rising pink."

"Well," said Katherine, "in this one Rapunzel didn't just let down her long hair."

"You're right," said the cat. "Rapunzel. That was her favorite story."

"The way you told it," said Bergen.

"Tell it," said God, leaning back and putting his feet up on the edge of the table.

"Well," said the cat, "Let's see if I can remember. The sun rose pink, hunh?"

"Yes," said Bergen. "And it circled the room where there was a girl, older than I was, of course."

"But you'll soon be as big as she," purred the cat.

"Your voice is all wrong, though," said Bergen, stroking the sleek black fur. "I miss your voice."

"This is my voice, Bergen. You have to get used to this!"

"I like your other one better, is all. I used to sit curled in Grandma's lap with her big, warm arms all around me, and I'd press my ear to her chest because she had this wonderful voice. A high, rumbly sort of voice. It was like I could feel the words forming inside of her, and then they'd come out of her mouth and circle to my other ear. 'The sun rose pink.' Just remembering those words is still enough to calm me right down."

"You take what you got, Bergen," said the cat. "You can't have it all ways."

"No, I guess not."

"So," said God. "You gonna tell the story or not?"

The cat stood on Bergen's lap, stretched, and climbed onto the table. Sitting in the middle, looking square at God, the cat said, "Do you know the story of Rapunzel?"

"Not really," said God.

"Well, it's kind of stupid to tell it to grown adults. Watch," said the cat as it slowly closed its eyes. Between its feet appeared a miniature scene: a wood-burning stove with red glowing rings on its black surface, a fat woman in a blue cotton dress kneading bread on a round table, a little girl with long blond hair stroking the big claw feet under the table. The woman brushed her hands, and flour dust floated down. The little girl poked her head out from under the table and stuck her tongue out under the falling powder. "Ahh! Gotcha!" said the woman, scooping the laughing child out from under the table, swinging her into her lap as she sat.

"This is great," said God.

"I learned it from you," said the cat.

"Grandma, Grandma," said the little girl. "Tell me a story."

"Which story, honey?" asked the woman, tucking the little girl into a ball in her arms.

"About the girl in the tower," said the little girl, pushing her ear into her grandma's chest.

"Well, the sun rose pink, and its softness circled the room where there was a girl, older than you, but you'll soon be as big as she. And this girl had long blond hair like you. So blond in fact that it was golden and shone all by itself in the darkness of the darkest night."

"Why's she in the tower, Grandma?"

"Well, honey, I'm not really sure. But she was in this tower, and the ones who put her there thought she was closed away and all alone. But at night the glow worms would dance for her, and two of her friends were hummingbirds, and they came to sing her songs. She was never really alone. But she was trapped in the tower, and, though she could see the pink gold of the sun circling all around the tower, she could never feel it shining on her.

"She was there for many years when one day a man came to the tower, but he didn't have a rope. So she let down her long hair, and he used it to pull himself up the tower to her."

"Ouch," said the little girl, scrunching up in her grandma's lap. "That would hurt so bad."

"Yes, honey, that did hurt. She thought she wanted the company, though. It'd been so many years that she'd been alone."

"What happened then?" asked the little girl, looking into her grandma's eyes.

"Well, they became close, and, for a time, it was good, but he began to use her and be mean to her, and she couldn't sleep nights anymore, and finally she lost her dreams, which were her only real freedom. So one day, what do you think she did?"

"I don't know. What?"

"Yes you do! She cut off all her hair!"

"All of it?" asked the little girl, squeezing tighter in her grandma's arms.

"Almost all until it was very short on her head. So that night, when he came and called, "Rapunzel, Rapunzel, let down your golden hair.'"

"You said long before."

"Long or golden, it doesn't matter, because what do you think she did?"

"Oh! She dropped her hair! Splat!"

"Down on his head!"

The child rolled into a ball of laughter.

"And then?" asked the woman.

"She weaved a cloth."

"A cloth of what?"

"Of glow worm thread!"

"That looked like?"

"Rainbows!" called the child.

"Yes, and the color of shells," said the woman. "The insides of shells. All spun together. Iridescent. That's what it was. Iridescent rainbow cloth woven from glow worm thread."

"And she made a parachute."

"Yes. And then the hummingbirds who were her friends came, and they held on to the cloth."

"And she held on too," cried the girl.

"And they took her out of the tower, through the window, flying past the forest, and out to sea. Her hair was like a golden cap, and her smile was bright as the sun, and she flew and flew and flew far away to the place where the dolphins play," said the grandma, hugging the little girl close.

They sat quiet for a bit, and then the woman said, "Time for bed, sugar, it's time to go to sleep. You look so sleepy." She hugged the child and stroked her cheek softly.

The child giggled. "Do more love fingers."

The woman stroked the cheek a bit more. Then she bent forward and brushed her eyelashes on the child's cheek.

"More butterfly kisses!" called the child.

"Enough now. Better get your toe-balls moving, or it'll soon be morning, and here we'll be, sitting here still, Bergen and me, sound asleep, rolled all up together like this."

The miniature woman picked up the little girl and carried her toward the door that stood by the cat's left paw.

"My sack full of potatoes. My saggy, sleepy doll," she said, kissing the little girl on the nose as the scene disappeared.

"That's sweet," said God.

"Yah," said Bergen. "They don't make grandmas like they used to."

The cat stretched. "They never made 'em like me. I was an original invention. That's what your grandpa used to say. 'With you, Nina, they broke the mold and threw away the key.' He was always mixing his metaphors like that. An interesting man, my Olaf. Worth coming home, I tell you. He made it worth coming home!"

"My Kristian doesn't? Is that what you mean?" asked Bergen.

"If he does, why then are you here?" The cat didn't wait for an answer. It jumped off the table and pranced with its tail and head erect straight out of the room.

"Quite a lady," said God.

"She used to be," said Bergen. "I don't know why I put up with her now."

"Old connections are tough to break," said Katherine.

"Thank goodness for that!" said Bergen as she hugged Katherine hard.

"Yep," said God. "Thank goodness for that!"

Just then the sun rose pink behind the mountain.

"Isn't that the West?" asked Katherine.

"It's Grandma. Up to her old tricks. Trying to make a point. She'll shake up everybody in town!" Bergen stomped toward the door and shouted, "Stop it! Keep your stories and reality straight. You'll confuse the natives."

God laughed until his belly puffed up like the Buddha's. "Not likely!" he said as he waddled toward the door. "It's all a play anyway, and we're all just dreamers."

"In somebody else's dream," said Katherine.

"With permission," said God, "I leave your dream."

"Permission granted," said Bergen.

"Then *adios*," said God.

"And *adieu*," said Bergen as she closed the door behind him. "*Adieu, mon cher, adieu.*"

30

"It was my art that kept me alive then," said Bergen.

"I can imagine," said Katherine. They sat on the floor in Bergen's studio, watching the slow moving sand sift through a crack under the window. "How old was he?"

"Seven. I always knew I would have him only 'til then, and, oddly, he seemed to know it, too." Bergen pried a floorboard free and lifted from the empty space below a lacquer box big enough to cup in her two hands. "He gave me his memories," she said. "I keep them in here." She lifted the lid and a child's thin voice sang, "Row, row, row your boat."

Before them, in the dim light of the studio, a young boy thrust his spade into sand. Hot sun beat down on his back.

"That's the beach near Marseilles, isn't it?" asked Katherine.

"Joey loved it there," said Bergen.

The water gleamed like hot silver, the sun basted Joey's small back with his sweat, and he bit his tongue as he stuck the blade hard into the sand. "I'm going to China, too!" he said as he scooped out a spadeful of dark, wet sand.

Water sprayed over him and dripped from his hair into the hole. "Hey!" he shouted and turned around.

A dolphin nodded in the water close to the beach. He seemed to be laughing, and Joey scrambled to his feet laughing, too.

"A dolphin!" he shouted across the water, clapping his hands, jumping up and down. "A dolphin!"

Joey waded into the water toward the animal, the wet rolling off his thin, tanned thighs like driplets of mercury, his hand outstretched. The dolphin dipped and chirped and bumped his nose against Joey's hand. "Bird beak!" cried Joey. The dolphin laughed as though he'd been tickled. Joey laughed, too.

"Funny dolphin. My mother painted you once. She found a picture in a book and painted you."

The scene faded and was replaced by one of a younger Bergen, paintbrush in hand, stroking gray against a tight-stretched canvas.

"They're kind," she was saying to Joey, who stood next to her watching the dolphin take shape against the rough surface. "They take care of people when they're hurt in the water. They care if you're sick, and they'll stay with you. They won't go away. Dolphins are kinder than people. More compassionate."

"What's com pash nut, mama?"

"Compassionate. Caring. They're kind in a way that helps you. Do you know that when a baby dolphin is born, it needs to have air to breathe? It would drown. So to help the baby so it won't drown, some of the other dolphins get around the mother and lift the baby up to the air."

"How do they do that? Do they have hands?"

"No. On their backs. They lift the baby up on their backs, together."

"Do dolphin mamas sing to their kids, too?"

"Maybe. What do you think they sing?"

"'Make New Friends'?"

"Maybe."

"I wish I was a dolphin."

"Me too. I wish we both were," she said. "Then we could swim all over the place together. *Monsieur Dauphin* and his mama."

Bergen and her easel faded and Joey splashed in the water again. "Together. Together. Are you my mama?" he asked the dolphin. "No, my mama, she's in China, far, far, far away." He circled his arms around the dolphin's body. "Can you take me to her?"

The dolphin nodded.

"Is China far? Do you know where to go?" Joey asked the dolphin.

An image of Bergen folding clothes into a satchel filled the studio space. "I'll tell you a secret," she said to Joey who sat on the big bed watching her.

"What secret?"

"I love you."

"That's not a secret! Everybody knows that. My grandmama knows and my grandpère knows and my Uncle Kristian knows."

"Do you know?"

"No."

"Remember this secret: even though I'm gone, I'm here, and I love you."

"But why do you have to go to that dish place?" Sadness filled the room like a flower wilting in the hot sun.

"China, Joey. China is a country like France. And don't worry—I won't be gone long," said Bergen.

"Can't I come?"

"Not this time."

"But I want to be with you, mama."

"You can't," she said. "Not this time." She snapped the satchel's mouth and buckled a leather belt around its middle. "It's time for bed now."

"Remember my dream, mama? I dreamed about that cloud that was eating people. Are you going there?"

The images broke like reflections on a pool scattered by a rock. Then a younger Bergen appeared holding a smaller Joey tightly, his pixie face bobbing through the candlelight circle as she rocked him, cooing, "Shh. It was just a dream. Clouds can't eat people. Shh, honey. It was just a dream. I'll sing you a song to make the bad dream go away. 'Mama's little baby like shortnin' shortnin' Mama's little baby likes shortnin' bread.'"

"Not that song, mama. I don't like that song."

"Shall I sing 'Summertime'?"

"No. Sing row row row your boat."

"Row row row your boat, gently down the stream,

merrily, merrily, merrily, merrily, life is but a dream."

"A good dream, mama? Is it a good dream?"

A spray of water shattered the candle circle, and Joey straddled the dolphin's back and soared over the waves. "To China!" he called into the spray. "China! Here we come, mama! Oh, but look, *Monsieur Dauphin.* The red bird!"

Above their heads flew a bright red bird, up high into a canopy of trees under which Bergen peddled a bike. Joey sat scrunched in a big basket wired to the handlebars, his head turned up toward the tree branches overhead, watching as the red bird swung through the trees.

"Mama," said Joey.

Peddle, peddle, puff, puff. "*Oui?*" Bergen's red face smiled back at him.

"Mama. I want to die when I'm seven. Is that all right? You could keep my bones. I could die at home in my bed, and you could keep my bones."

"Bones."

"Bones."

"Bones."

The word echoed in the empty room. "We never found his bones," said Bergen as she closed the box lid.

Katherine put an arm around her shoulder.

"I should have been there," said Bergen. "Not off in China fighting a revolution. I should have been at home." She dropped her forehead to the slick surface of the oriental box, and she cried.

Kristian arrived the next day, but only God was there to meet him. Bergen and Katherine had left before sunrise for the canyon.

"Bergie, are you here? Bergie?"

God sat at the table sipping coffee. "You looking for Bergen?"

"Who are you?"

"You must be her old man."

"Is she here?"

"Naw, they left before sunrise for the canyon. Have some coffee, man."

Kristian turned in a circle looking around the kitchen. "Who's they?"

"She and that girl she used to know named Katherine."

"I don't know any Katherine."

"Someone who died the day you two met, that's all I know," said God.

"What nonsense you talk," said Kristian. "If she's dead, how can she be with Bergie? Where'd you say they went?"

God floated him a picture of Katherine and Bergen walking through steep cliffs along a dry arroyo bed.

"How'd you do that? Is that some kind of a projector?"

Bergen stopped and looked back the way they'd come. She said something to the fat girl with her, but Kristian couldn't hear. "Can't you turn up the volume."

"Naw," said God. "That's invasion of privacy. Going too far, you know. People've got a right to their privacy, don't you think?"

"I don't know what you're talking about," said Kristian. "You don't live here, too, do you?"

"Naw. Me and my coyotes live next door. C'mon. I'll show you." God set down his cup and climbed through the kitchen window.

"Isn't there a door?"

God stuck his head back through the window. "Yeah. The back one over there takes you to my house. But you get there faster by the window."

"Can I leave my suitcase here?"

"Who'd take it?"

Kristian looked at him suspiciously. "It's got some very valuable things in it."

"Then no one will take it. But if you're worried, give it to me. I'll carry it." God tried to take the suitcase, but Kristian grabbed the handle with both hands and pulled it tight to his belly.

"I got it," he said. "Where's the door?"

God pointed to the wall and a hole appeared. "Take that. It'll get you to my house almost as fast as the window."

Kristian looked over his shoulder and back at God. He

sidled backward, his suitcase handle pushed so tight into his solar plexus that his words came like air from a bellows. "I think I'll wait by the front door."

"Suit yourself. I'll be here if you need me. And I'll know if you do."

Kristian slipped into a chair by the front door, his eyes fixed on the dreadlocks. "No. That's okay."

"How about some entertainment then? It'll be a long wait. They're going to be gone for a few days."

"A few days?"

"At least."

Kristian dropped his head to the suitcase that stood on his lap.

"You're right," said God. "You shouldn't have come."

"How'd you know what I was thinking?"

"Why wouldn't I know? Look, don't worry. There's plenty to do. Try this for awhile. I'll be back."

Three parachutes floating like dark moons in a night sky appeared where God had been. "Ahh!" belched Kristian. Italy stretched its deep fields under his feet. He heard the sound of a tank rolling through the dark, and he dropped into a furrow, tucking his face under his black-sleeved arm. "Please," he whispered. "I don't want to be here!" The tank consumed the silence, swallowed the shush of parachute silk, beat the earth into a kettledrum's pulse. Kristian felt the dirt dancing in and out of his nostrils with each fierce blow. His head filled with the cry, "Home, God, please."

The noise stopped, heat buzzed around him, and light

teased its way under Kristian's arm. He peeked out. There in a corona a hand pointed from a man's shadowed shape. "Ah!" screamed Kristian, throwing his arm out toward the shape. "I died!"

"How about a cold one?" asked God as he slapped a bottle of beer into Kristian's hand.

"Am I dead?"

"Not that I know of, though I reckon your wife could answer that better than me."

Kristian sat up and took a long pull on the bottle. "I thought I was dead!"

"Nope."

"Where am I then?" He looked around him at the newspapers stacked around tables and at chairs overflowing with dishes and beer bottles.

"Be it ever so humble," said God, "there's no place like home."

"You can say that again." He sucked on his upturned bottle. "You wouldn't have any more of these, would you?"

"There's a cooler behind you."

Kristian got himself another beer, cleared a space on the couch, and settled carefully next to a sprung spring. God's coyotes formed a half-ring in front of him. "Boy," said Kristian. "I really thought for a moment there I was dead."

God dropped into a chair next to the couch. "I felt that way in Nam more than once."

"You were in Vietnam?"

"Twice. Extended my hitch both times. The worst part

was always the nights, laying in them rocking hammocks, smelling the noises all around you. Enemy smelt like smoke and camphor in Nam. It was like a mouth taste when they was coming. That and the smell of crushed plants. Sometimes you'd lay there rocking, and you could swear you'd hear them plants crying when they was stepped upon. Hand me a beer, would ya?"

Kristian lifted the cooler lid. "Mind if I help myself to one more?"

"It's a never-ending supply. Have all you want." God took the bottle from Kristian and used his back teeth to pry off the bottle cap. He spit it into the half-ring of coyotes. They ignored it.

Kristian twisted the cap from the bottle and stuck it in his pocket. The beer went down smooth, like oil. "What've you done since Vietnam?"

"They've locked me up a few times in Vegas."

"Locked you up in Las Vegas? What'd you do? Cheat at blackjack?"

"Forgot you're not from here, man. The first Vegas. Las Vegas, New Mexico. Mental institution there, you know. No, they locked me up there for awhile. Always let me out again, though. I come home, and it's okay, but I always get a hankering to leave here. And then they lock me up, you know. So I stay in Vegas for awhile, and then come back here."

Kristian looked out the window at the few creosote bushes holding the chalky earth. "What would you come back here for?"

"This is home. A man's gotta come home. It's the only place he belongs really, you know."

"It's a funny place to think of as home."

"Well, as my old dad used to say, 'Variety is the spice of life, and difference makes the world go round.' To each his own. Live and let live, right?"

"I guess," said Kristian. He took a slug of his beer without taking his eyes off God.

"So, what'd you say you do?"

"Didn't say," said Kristian. "I'm mostly retired right now, but, and you probably won't believe this, I was an embalmer and a mortician since about '50. Yeah, I guess it was '50. December the 9th, 1950. I should remember that day. My father's birthday, and was actually the day he died, too. My pa was like that. Liked to tie up all the ends. Leave nothing unfinished. That was my pa, the way he was. But you don't want to hear this."

"Sure. Have another beer."

Kristian reached for the bottle and said, "Well, if you want to, I guess there's no harm in it. It's like this: he died a couple years before. Shot himself. So when it came time to start my own business, I thought, 'What better tribute?' I had my first cemetery then, too. So I had them send him over. He was in Norway. Buried in his hometown. Had them ship him. He was my first interment. It was a nice affair. Bergie can tell you all about it. She was there. We'd been married for going on eight years then. Still got the cemetery, of course. Don't do any embalming now. Getting too old. What of your pa? Where's he buried? Or is he still living?"

"Oh, that old man lives on and on. There's no getting rid of him."

The coyotes roared with laughter, and Kristian jumped and landed on the sprung spring. He checked his trousers for a rent. "When'd you say Bergie was going to be back?"

God grinned and stuck his tongue through the gap in his smile. "Few days," said the biggest coyote.

"How'd you do that?" asked Kristian. "Are you a ventriloquist, too?"

"Naw, it's the old coyote. He seems to like you. Maybe you knew him somewhere, sometime."

"Knew him? How would I have known a coyote?"

"I'll take you to her if you want," said the coyote.

Kristian's eyes got big, and he pressed back against the couch. "Coyotes can't talk. You're throwing your voice."

"He couldn't throw his voice if he tried," said the coyote. "But, seriously. I could take you to her if you want."

"Don't go with him," said God. The coyote turned and glared at him. "And don't give me the evil eye. I know you're up to no good."

"What you know you should keep to yourself," said the coyote. "I don't know why you're always meddling in everyone else's business. In all the years I've known you, you've always got to be in the middle of everything. Just butt out!" He turned his head back to Kristian. "So, what you say? Want to go?"

"No," said Kristian looking from God to the coyote and back again. "No. I think I'll just wait here for Bergie to get back." He slid out of the couch, leaning back, away from the coyote, and said to God, "There must be a good motel in town?"

"Sure. I'll take you there."

"No," said Kristian, grabbing his suitcase, backing up toward what looked like a door. "If you'll just point me the way, I can get there on my own."

"That wouldn't be wise," said God. "There are some strange people walking around this town at night. I'll take you. It'll be safer that way." He walked past Kristian to the door, opened it, and bowed, sweeping his arm to show Kristian the way. "After you."

Kristian looked out into the dark night. "No," he said. "Maybe you better go first."

The coyotes followed them out the door.

Sand slid down the sides of the canyon, slithering over the dry arroyo bed into the footprints left by Katherine and Bergen's bare feet. The wind followed, flipping their skirts like a naughty schoolboy. An army of lizards walked beside.

"Don't they ever bother you?" asked Katherine.

"Shhhh!" said Bergen. The sun circled her head like bees.

Farther along the arroyo, the walls moved closer and closer together until they squeezed out the sun. Bergen stopped. The silence wrapped them in its breath, and Katherine felt as though she were falling, falling, falling through the quiet, her parachute shushing above her. She opened her mouth into a loud 'O,' but it fell unsaid into the sand. Bergen kicked it into a pile of sticks and scorched Katherine with a look as bright as a bomb flowering in a moonless sky. Katherine sank, covering her eyes with her hands. Some lizards flipped out from under her skirt where the billowing, settling cloth had trapped them. They climbed her knee and stuck out twenty small tongues, which Katherine couldn't see because her eyes were squeezed tight under the flutter of her hands.

Suddenly she felt herself rise, felt the lizards cling with sharp claws to her skirt, and she peeked through her fingers. There beside her Bergen sat crosslegged on top of five feet of air. Katherine straightened her own legs, but the movement flipped her onto her back. She floated beside Bergen, her eyes screaming, "Help." Bergen motioned her away and began floating upward toward an opening in the canyon face as wide as Katherine's 'O.' When she reached the black circle, she floated through it. Katherine lay on her back, the lizards clinging to her legs and stomach, her skirt hanging down behind. She couldn't move—couldn't go up or down—so she floated in the silence and tried to forget falling. Hours passed, and the night closed around her like a wing. She was afraid, but there was nothing she could do.

"It's like dying," she thought, and the memory of Bergen's shoes' chorus paraded through her mind. "Falling."

No!

"Falling."

No!

"Falling down."

Noooooooooo!

Air rushed past her, crushed into waves by the blur of propellers.

What am I doing? Why would I be standing out here—on an airplane wheel—gonna jump, ready to jump. I don't believe I'm doing this—only a fool would be doing this, could be doing this. Jump and live, jump thousands of feet and live. Back in, no, back in, crawling in, he won't let me back in. Bastard—fool—the plane'll crash, sure, the plane'll crash.

But that wasn't her memory, was it? She hadn't been frightened. She'd soared from that plane, falling like Frederick, calling "One one thousand, two one thousand," feeling the air tickle into her nostrils as she fell in the dark as in a dream. No. It wasn't she. It was Bergen. Bergen who clung to the struts, who wouldn't jump, who looked back into the plane with eyes like hooks that would keep her from falling. Frederick had pushed, pushed her gently at first, then firmly. "Go," he screamed against the wind. "Jump now." But Bergen had looped her eyes around Katherine's, pulled tight with her "Help!" as she fell forward, away from the door, pushed by Frederick's pianist hands.

Katherine jumped after her, down, down, down into Bergen's memory.

Water running in the bathroom woke Bergen. Pulling the pillow over her head, she fought for sleep, losing, angry. Noise from the bathroom continued, warming the morning's hard grayness. Bergen, defeated, lay tracing her irritation, gouging it deeper, counting the mornings lost—dreams lost. Katherine's house.

"My house!" thought Katherine. "That little house in the country by the border. I'd forgotten about that! And it even had a bathtub! What a luxury. That bathtub with its spigot placed just right! I'd slip down through the steam, the water easing away the night's hold. Slipping forward 'til my toes smoothed the spigot, sliding down toward the rushing water. I was in Bali. The heat caressed me, enveloping me, warm. The sun was shining on my bare skin, my golden, freckled heat-warm skin. Sky rich with color behind the deep heights of the mountains. I lay on the sand, warm, fine grains running through my hand. An hourglass of uncaptured time—me the island the sun. So warm the water. I eased my body forward—the gentleness lapped against my thighs, up stroking my belly, up sliding over my back as I dipped my breasts, breaking the water's tightness. I rolled back, my hair flowed out from my body, silk strands fluting the water, weaving my skin. Wrapping my body, holding me so softly, floating in the water warm with sun. Through the water pulsed a drum song, womb beat echoed back to my ears. Up through my hands where they rested on the smooth rounding of my still hot thigh. Pulsing, soothing, calling me home. Quiet warm water, rock me gently, gently. Oh."

Bergen shouting through the bathroom door, "Aren't you done yet? Damn it, Katherine, every morning!"

Bergen sitting at the table, face winced against the morning's pain, attacking a sheet of paper, burying it under pastel crayons.

Katherine asking, "A new painting?"

Bergen ignoring her, scrubbing black over the shapes and lines.

49

Katherine cutting a piece of bread.

Bergen saying, "I'm not jumping."

"You have to jump! They're counting on us! You can't back out now."

Bergen's face, frightened, listening. Her eyes, strange yellow eyes, shot through with fear now. Eyes dulling against Katherine's words, turning inward, hearing nothing. Bergen's face crushed white against her words.

What if the parachute didn't open? The reserve, would it work? She stood clawing the strut, fighting her terror. She must jump, she couldn't jump, she couldn't get back in. Frederick, kneeling in the door, screamed through the wind ripping past her, "Jump now!"

Bergen falling like the weight of sleep into Katherine's arms. Katherine helping her to the bed, lying with her on the bed, soothing her. Holding her in her arms, mother arms, rocking Bergen softly, singing. Singing old, mother songs. Stroking the light, soft head cradled on her breast, ear pressed to her heart—soothing sound, heart song.

"When you were a little girl, Bergen, you used to laugh, and laugh, and laugh. Mama used to tell you stories. Funny stories, or silly stories, or call you funny names. You liked that, when your mama called you names, funny names. How you could laugh! Your mama can hear you laughing still. Your mama can't remember anything better than Bergen laughing."

Bergen closing tight on the bed.

Katherine asking, "Can't I get you some tea?"

Shaking her head, eyes closing like shades.

"A bath, that'd make you feel better."

Pulling her cold hand from Katherine's and thinking, "The fire needs wood."

Katherine saying, "The fire needs wood. It's cold today."

Bergen turning away from her, falling into sleep.

You can't make me do it. "You either live or you die," *he said.* "You won't have to worry about it if it doesn't open," *he said. That's what I'm afraid of. It's a long way dooooooown.*

Bergen walking into the kitchen, her face a mask in the late afternoon light.

Katherine asking, "Eat? Do you want to eat?"

"Yes. Pancakes. Like my momma used to make."

"On Saturdays, special days, when you were little?"

"No. Before she died." Bergen caving in then, dropping to the floor, laughing. Laughing her child laugh—rare tinkling sounds coming from way down. "Same age as me, Katherine. She was the same age as me." Deep, haunted echoes, laughter long forgotten, rolling through her.

She automatically pushed off, kicking back with her feet, casting her hands from the struts, sailing backwards into the iced wind. Graceful, the pilot said later, her body arched, arms wide, legs spread. Freefall counting, "One one thousand, two one thousand." Falling.

Katherine falling to the floor, laughing too, and she landed, "thumph," on the dry sand bed, and the lizards scattered around her.

It was night, and the moon lipped over the steep canyon wall, sending silver slipping over its sides. The sand was cold under Katherine's bare legs.

Bergen floated down from the 'O' to the earth and took Katherine's hand. "Let's go home," she said in the quiet of Katherine's mind. "Home."

"Have you seen the cemetery, Bergie? It's a shambles," said Kristian, leaning against the door jamb in Bergen's studio.

Bergen shoved her face closer to the canvas. "Damn eyes! They get dimmer every day."

"Did you hear what I said, Bergie?"

"Not now, Kristian. Can't you see I'm trying to paint?" She touched the brush bristles to her tongue, moistened them, then dabbed the brush in a blob of white acrylic.

"Bergie, I've told you not to do that! That's plastic. You're coating your stomach with plastic."

"Maybe that's why I can eat chile, and you can't. Here. Try a lick." She held the brush toward him.

He crossed his arms over his chest and looked at the ceiling. "I was trying to tell you about the cemetery."

"What cemetery?" asked Bergen as she leaned close to the canvas and laid a fine white line along the edge of a wave.

"You never listen to me!"

"I'm listening," said Bergen as she scraped at the white with her ragged pinkie fingernail.

"Stop a minute," said Kristian. "Sit down. Have a cup

of coffee. I want to tell you about this cemetery."

Bergen sighed, put her brush behind her ear, and followed Kristian into the kitchen.

"I made some fresh," said Kristian as he poured her a cup of coffee. "Sit. Fresh with eggshells. You always forget to put the eggshells in. That's why yours is so bitter, you know."

"I don't want to fight with you, Kristian. Just tell me about the graveyard." She sat at the table and cleared a space among the dishes left from breakfast.

"Cemetery, Bergie! Graveyard sounds so . . . "

"So real?"

"No, so spooky, I guess. Good coffee, hunh?"

Bergen took a sip and burned her tongue. "You don't have to boil it!"

"Yes, you do, or it's no good. How many times have I told you?"

"Oh, let's see: at least once a week for—how long's it been I've been putting up with you?"

"Since '42! You know the date exactly."

"How could I forget?"

They huddled in the barn. Not in the hayloft. That was the first place the soldiers always looked. No, they huddled together back of the troughs, where time had etched a space under the stone wall. The tanks shook mortar loose, and it fell like heavy rain around them. They huddled together, close to one another, Kristian's arms tight around Bergen, whose eyes were filled with the sight of two limp bodies hanging in the trees.

"We have to get out of here," whispered Kristian. "Once they find those bodies, we're dead."

Bergen sat staring, not moving.

"Come on!" Kristian hissed. He stood and pulled her by the hand, but she was a dead weight. "Now!" he commanded as he slapped her hard across the face.

"What did you say?" asked Bergen.

"Now," said Kristian. "We have to do something about it now."

"About what?"

"The cemetery! Haven't you been listening to a word I've been saying? The cemetery is in disarray, and it's almost All Soul's. I figure as long as I'm stuck here, I might as well do something about it. But I can't do it by myself. It's too much work."

"Kristian, why don't you just go back?" said Bergen as she traced patterns in toast crumbs left on a cracked plate.

Kristian collected the china from the table and settled it gently in the sink. He sunk the trap into the drain, turned on the hot water, squirted detergent into the stream, and watched the bubbles grow.

"I said," said Bergen, "why don't you just go home?"

Kristian neatly rolled his white shirt sleeves and sunk his hands into the steaming, bubbling water. He slowly washed each dish and rinsed it under the tap. Then he released the water from the sink, wiped his hands on the linen towel he'd bought at the Coast to Coast store, and rolled his sleeves back down, buttoning each cuff. When he was done, he sat down next to Bergen, took her hand, and played with her ring, circling her diamond engagement ring around and around her finger. Finally he said, "That cemetery, Bergie. It really does need to be done."

"All right, old man! We'll clean the cemetery. When? When do you want to do it?"

"Today," said Kristian. "This afternoon."

"Too soon. I'm painting today. Tomorrow. Tomorrow morning."

"No. Today."

"Why can't it wait one day?"

"At this age, Bergie, you think we got one day to wait? If we don't do it today, how do you know we don't die tonight? Then who'll do it?"

"You're impossible! How should I know? Why should I care? I'm painting. But you'll just nag me to death if I don't help you today, won't you?"

Kristian twirled her diamond in slow circles. "It's a nice stone. My father got it in Africa."

"I know."

"They don't cut stones like that anymore. Look at all the rainbows it makes. That's good cutting."

Bergen looked into Kristian's glasses and saw Joey's reflection on their surface. She spun around fast.

"What?" said Kristian. "You look like you've seen a ghost."

The room was empty; the midday sun was oozing through the barely open window; Kristian's breathing crinkled in his throat.

Bergen looked back at Kristian, squeezed his hand. "I'll get my friends. We'll meet you there."

"I already talked to John. He'll come."

"Who's John?"

"What do you mean, 'Who's John?'"

"I mean, 'Who's John?'" said Bergen, snatching her hand away.

Kristian laughed. "You mean you been buying burritos from this guy, and all the time he's got you fooled?"

"*El Malo*?"

"Can't you speak English, Bergie? We're not in a foreign country, you know."

Bergen sat with her shoulders hunched, her hands twisted in her lap, watching the movies reel back in her mind. "You're right!" she said finally. "It is *El Diablo*!"

"The same!" said Kristian. "Remember when he broke us out of jail?"

"I'd rather forget, thanks."

"Your nemesis, right here in town!"

"Where'd you run into him?" asked Bergen.

"In the cemetery. I saw him and your Katherine smooching on top of the sarcophagus of one of the town's leading lights."

"Katherine?"

"That's what I thought. What does he see in her? Course some men like a handful. Me, I always liked them lithe," he said, stroking Bergen's hip.

"Not now, Kristian! Let me think."

"That's right. Always did like John a bit yourself, didn't you?"

"Not hardly! Imagine, *El Diablo* here in town."

Kristian stood and tucked his shirttails down into his trousers. "So, we'll meet you there, at the cemetery, at, say, two?"

"*El Diablo!*" said Bergen.

"Bergie, don't forget. Two."

"Oh, what?" asked Bergen, pushing back her hair. "Two. Right. The clock will remind me. Two."

"God isn't here," said the biggest coyote.

Bergen stuck her head through the doorway and looked around the junk-cluttered room.

"He isn't. Believe me," said the coyote.

"Do you know then when he'll be back?"

"I'm not his keeper," he said, flipping his tail and turning into the room. "How should I know?"

"Did he say anything before he left?"

"Not to me," said the coyote as he settled on the couch next to the sprung spring. He crossed his legs. "He doesn't much confide in me these days."

"Who would know?"

"You could try old John."

"The burrito man?"

"Is there any other john in town?" asked the coyote with a snigger.

Bergen closed the door and picked her way through the can-strewn yard. "Owwh!" cried her shoes when she stepped on some glass.

"Sorry," said Bergen. "Damn eyes are getting so weak, it's hard to see the ground anymore."

"Why don't you get glasses?" asked her shoes.

"How about a new pair of eyes, instead?"

"That could be arranged," said the shoes as they winced at the devil's claw that sprung up, pointing its talons straight toward their soft blue leather.

"Maybe I'm just a bit afraid of what I'll see," said Bergen as she lowered herself to the flagstone stoop by the back door. "God's gone; Katherine's with *El Malo*; the coyotes are too lazy to even bother asking. Who else can I get to help?"

"What do you need?" asked her shoes.

"Oh, I told Kristian I'd get some people to help clean up the graveyard."

"Count us out," said her left shoe.

"Why?" asked her right shoe. "It might be fun."

"I'm not going near a graveyard, and that's final," said the left.

"Well, I'll go," said the right. "You can count on me."

"Thanks," said Bergen.

"Not on me!" said the left.

"I wish I knew where God was," said Bergen as the shrill ring of the phone pierced the back door. She ran in and lifted the receiver from the hook.

"Wondering where I am?" asked God.

"Yes, as a matter of fact. How'd you know?" asked Bergen. She sat on the counter and dangled her legs, bumping her heels against the wood. "Where in the world are you?"

"In Vegas."

"Las Vegas?"

"The other one. Ask Kristian. He knows all about it."

"I can't ask him. He's over at the graveyard."

"I know. I meant to help him with that, but I got sort of antsy to see some friends of mine up north, you know. Well, D.H. and me got into a fight in Taos, you see . . . "

"D.H.?"

"Yeah, Lawrence, you know, and we was fighting over . . . "

"But Lorenzo's dead!"

"So some say, but as I was saying, we got into this fight, and—well it's a long story. To make it short, here I am, back in slick city, where the world's white and the walls, soft. Can you spring me?"

"Get you out, you mean?" asked Bergen, who'd stopped bumping her heels and was leaning forward to hear God better.

"Exactly! If you could get my bicycle out of the shed and bring that too, I'd be ever appreciative."

"But where are you?"

"Gotta go!" whispered God. "They're coming to get me."

The line went dead. Bergen held the phone out from her ear and stared at the mouthpiece as though she could find God there. "What in the world?" she said aloud.

"You shoulda known that guy was a nut," said her shoes.

"Shhh!" said Bergen. She dug in a drawer and pulled out an atlas. "Las Veeeeeegas," she said as she dragged her finger over the index. "Oh, there is more than one!"

"More than one what?" asked Katherine as she walked

into the kitchen. "Got any food? I'm famished."

"I don't know if I should talk to you," said Bergen.

"What are you so huffy about?"

"As if you didn't know!"

"No, I don't," said Katherine as she dug through the icebox. "Any mayonnaise in the house?"

"You never liked mayonnaise," said Bergen.

"Different life, different likes."

"I guess! Can't imagine what you see in the devil himself."

"John, you mean?"

"Don't be coy with me! You know exactly of whom I speak."

"Oh, aren't we proper! 'Of whom I speak'! Well, if you mean John, I think that's my business."

Bergen closed the book. "God's up in a place in Las Vegas. Locked up. Says Kristian knows something about it. We've got to get him out."

"How?" asked Katherine.

"He says to bring his bicycle."

"No, I mean, how do we get there? Las Vegas is a long way away."

Bergen opened the book again. "We could walk."

Katherine leaned over the map, her right hand on Bergen's left shoulder. "Oh! A different Las Vegas. Look," she said, pointing to the map. "There's a train line running up that way. Isn't there a depot down by the river?"

"You're right," said Bergen following the cross marks

up and across the page. "The Santa Fe line. I don't think they carry passengers on that line anymore."

"Then let's hop a freight!" said Katherine.

"I'm not going," said the left shoe.

"Well, I am!" said the right.

"A freight, hummmm?" Bergen eyes pulsed like fireflies. "I haven't done that in years."

"C'mon," said the right shoe to the left. "A little adventure never hurt anyone!"

"I've got an image to maintain," said the left.

"I need you both," said Bergen. "So, shush!"

The left shoe huffed. "You'll take me kicking and screaming all the way."

"So be it!" said Bergen as she dug through the drawer for some paper. "Why don't we ever have anything to write on in this house?"

"What do you need it for?" asked Katherine.

Bergen emptied out the drawer on the table and sifted through its contents. "Not a pencil even."

"What do you you need it for?"

"To leave Kristian a note," said Bergen as she walked out of the room.

"Why do you need to leave Kristian a note?" asked Katherine as she followed Bergen into her studio.

"Because," she said as she looked through the drawers of a large credenza, "there's a freight at noon. I hear it every day. We've got time to catch it, but not if we go by the graveyard, and I told him we'd be there to help at two."

"Don't we need him to get God out?" asked Katherine.

Bergen took a stretched canvas from a pile leaning against the wall and sat it on her easel. With some watered down black acrylic, she brushed the words: "Gone to get God—Back Soon."

"I said don't we need Kristian's help to get God out?"

"You know he wouldn't come anyway. Those two don't get along," said Bergen as she carried the canvas into the kitchen and propped it on the counter.

"He's going to be mad," said the left shoe.

"Shush!" said Bergen. "We're going, and I don't want to hear any more from you."

"Well," said Katherine, "I'll throw some things in a bag and run over and get John. We'll meet you in the copse north of the station, okay?"

"North?" asked Bergen absentmindedly as she followed Katherine to the closet.

"In the woods," said Katherine, stuffing clothes into a carry-on bag. "Can you get the bike there by yourself?"

"No, you better take it," said Bergen. "I'll find Grandma and see if I can get the coyotes to come."

"Okay. I'm gone. See you at noon," said Katherine as she ran to the door.

"Oh!" Bergen called after her. "Get Frederick. If he's in the plaza, tell him to come."

"Right!" said Katherine as she ran out the door.

"John, John, John! Why would she be bringing John?" mumbled Bergen as she packed her own clothes.

The material caught under her ragged fingernails, yet still she stroked it in the dark. "Frederick, Katherine," she whispered over and over as though their names would bring them back to her. She could feel truck vibrations through the dirt floor. "Katherine, Frederick," she whispered as she crawled the perimeter of the small box, checking along the interstice of wall and floor, clawing at any loose dirt. "Frederick, Katherine. Frederick. Frederick. Katherine."

Suddenly, a line colored like light through flesh hissed along the wall opposite the door. Bergen backed away, pushing hard against the door as the light burned its pattern through her closed eyes, onto her retinas.

Hissssssssssssssssssssssssss

Bergen squeezed her hands tight over her ears, but still the sound seeped into her bones, turned them to molten sludge.

Then the hiss stopped, and she opened her eyes as a gloved hand peeled back the wall like it was prying the lid off a tin can. The hand reached into the dark, grabbed one of the arms Bergen held tightly crossed over her chest, and pulled her through the gaping hole with the force of a machine. Her clothes caught on the sides of the gap, threads wrenching the metal into a cry.

"Oh, it's you!" hissed a man as thin as a shadow. "Where's he?"

"Who?" Bergen's voice gurgled up through a throat closed tight as wrung laundry.

Great hands shook her by the shoulders. "Don't play dumb. We got no time, broad. Where is he?" spat the shadow. "The guy with you. Where'd they put him?"

"I don't know."

"Tell me!"

She whimpered softly.

"Stay here!" The sound of his words sizzled around Bergen, and she tucked herself back into the box, pressed back, tight, against the door. "Frederick, Katherine, Frederick, Katherine," she whispered faster and faster, over and over. Then there was a creak of metal and Kristian whispering, "Come on!" She crawled toward his voice and into his arms.

"Leave her!" hissed the shadow as it bled back into the dark.

Kristian whispered in Bergen's ear: "The dogs are drugged, but we must hurry!" He pulled her along the edge of darkness to a truck parked just behind the floodlights that surrounded the guardhouse.

"*Heil Hitler!*" said the shadow's voice.

Bergen froze.

Kristian tugged her toward the back of the truck, and they both slipped under the tarp as another voice barked back in German.

Bergen started to speak, but Kristian clamped his hand tight against her mouth.

"*Heil Hitler!*" said the shadow's voice next to the tarp.

Heels clicked. "*Heil Hitler!*"

The truck door creaked, and the driver's side drooped with the weight of someone settling on the seat. The engine turned, caught, and the truck lurched forward, Kristian and Bergen sliding toward the tail as the floodlights oozed green through the tarp. For about a mile, the truck moved slowly, but when the dark swallowed them again, the driver screamed "Aiiee!" and gunned the motor and drove the truck into the potholes with neck-jarring speed.

Kristian sat up in the truck bed, returned the cry, and shouted into the wind "*El Diablo* did it again!"

"*El Diablo*?" asked Bergen.

"Who's *El Diablo*?" asked the cat as it dipped its claw in Bergen's suitcase and lifted a sweater. "And where are you going?"

"Us," said Bergen. "You, too. And we don't have time to talk if we're going to hop the noon freight."

"Great!" said the cat. "I haven't been on a train in years. Lifetimes, in fact. Why, I remember . . . "

"Grandma! Not now," said Bergen. "We don't have time for your stories. We've got to round up the coyotes and meet the others in fifteen minutes."

"Only one way to do that," said the cat as it followed Bergen out the back door. On the stoop, the cat let loose a high-pitched whistle through its bared teeth.

"Yaaaa!" cried all the coyotes as they appeared outside God's door.

"What'd you do that for?" asked the biggest as he rubbed his ears.

"God's locked up," said Bergen.

"So, what's new?" asked the coyote as he headed back into the house.

"We need your help to get him out," said Bergen.

"So, what's in it for me?"

"Ever hop a freight?" asked the cat.

"No, and why would I want to?"

"A little odyssey, maybe," said the cat.

"I don't go in for that literature stuff," he said, walking back into the house.

"Adventure!" cried the right shoe.

"Dementia!" cried the left.

"Dementia, hunh?" said the coyote poking his head out the door. "That might be interesting. How about it, fellas? A little trip?"

"Yeah . . . sure . . . why not?" said the coyotes.

A distant train whistle stirred a dust devil in the yard.

"C'mon," shouted Bergen as she grabbed the cat and hopped into the whirlwind's center. It sped toward the station with the coyotes loping behind.

Bergen watched the bright blue bowl of the sky as she leaned back against the coal car's sloping wall, the wind spinning against her like a tunneled wave, her bare toes wiggling, her shoes curled in her lap.

"Grandma," she asked, "do you remember the story about the old woman miner who broke through the roof of the sky?"

"Can't say that I do," said the cat as it tried to balance on the bike that lay in the center of the coal car. A paw slipped off the frame and touched the floor. "Eeaah!" it said, shaking its paw. "This car is so filthy!"

"Puss is afraid," said the biggest coyote. "'Fraid of a little dirt. Ain't that cat just the biggest adventurer you guys ever heard of?"

"Yeah . . . you bet . . . sure, is!" said the other coyotes as they stretched farther over the edge of the coal car, each trying to be the first to spot a train kill.

"I'm sure you told me that story," said Bergen.

Frederick swooped down from the car's edge and landed on the bike's spinning front wheel. It carried him round and round in slow circles, and he hopped the fork with each revolution. "Naw, you used to dream that one,

Bergen," he said as he circled. "Jeez, it's fun to be a bird! Don't know why I didn't do this earlier."

"Maybe if Katherine had come back as a bird, she'd be with us now, and not in the arms of that degenerate!" said Bergen.

"They tried, Bergen!" said the cat. "He really tried to get her on the train, but it was going too fast."

"Sure!"

"I don't know what you have against him anyway," said the cat. "They seem a cute couple."

"Little do you know!"

"There's one, there's one!" shouted the coyotes as they hopped from the car.

"Would someone get them back in here before that old bull in the caboose gets wise to us. I don't want to end up in jail, too," said Bergen.

The cat let loose another high-pitched whistle, and the coyotes came bounding over the walls just as Bergen snatched the cat from the bike.

"Now, behave!" said Bergen to the coyotes who glared at the cat.

Frederick still rode round and round on the spinning tire. "Why don't you tell us the story? I forget how it goes," he said.

"When'd I tell it to you?"

"Guess the first time was when I got back from Spain. That's when you and Katherine were still in Paris, I think."

"No, I hadn't met Katherine yet then," said Bergen. "*You* introduced us. Don't you remember?"

"Did I ever tell you where I met her?"

"At *Sacre Coeur*, wasn't it?"

"Not hardly! *Place Pigale* it was. *O la la!*"

"I don't want to know!"

"I do," said the cat.

"No," said Bergen. "I don't want to talk about Katherine right now."

"So, tell the story then," said the cat as it curled around the shoes in Bergen's lap. "I could use a few fresh ones."

"I don't know if I remember it all."

"It'll come," said Frederick. "I'll help you. Shared remembering."

"Well, okay," said Bergen as she stretched her sweaty legs out toward the bike. She could feel the coal dust ooze up over her calves. "Once upon a time . . . "

"That's a clever way to start!" said the cat.

"We can't all be as good as you," said Bergen. "Once upon a time there was this old woman miner who with her crew dug so deep into the depths of a mountain that she broke through the bowl of the sky."

"Bergen, that's awful!" said the cat. "You can't just hop into the story like that! You've got to build suspense!"

"She never could tell a good story," said Frederick.

"What do you want? I'm a painter. I never said I was a storyteller. Grandma was stingy with her genes."

"Well, the trick, Bergen," said the cat, "is you show, not tell."

"I don't know how to do that without a paintbrush in

my hand."

"Well, I imagine it's the same thing—except you're painting a picture with your words is all."

"Ah, for Pete's sake! Just let her tell the story," said the biggest coyote. "It'll probably be boring, but it'll help pass the time."

All the other coyotes howled and clapped their paws: "Story! Story!" they crooned.

"Okay," said Bergen, crossing her legs up under her full skirt. "This mountain, as I recall, was inhabited by all sorts of wondrous creatures. They lived within the mountain, and the earth pulsed with their breathing, but no one from the top side had ever seen them.

"There were many of these creatures living together under the mountain, and they had lived there from the beginning of time. They didn't know they were under a mountain, though. The underside of the mountain they called the sky. They never knew they were trapped like that, inside its dome, and they went on with their lives, with the seasons and changes brought by the rise and fall of sun and the moon under the dark, full dome.

"Those on the other side went on with their living, too, never knowing that any existed but them. Sometimes they'd drill their way into the mountain, but they never got far enough to drill past the dark bowl of sky.

"That is—not until one day. One day a coal-mining crew was digging deep into the mountain, deeper than they'd ever been before, and they broke through to the other side! The leader, an old woman, white hair bright

73

around her coal-darkened face, put her head through the opening where the space broke through. She couldn't believe what she saw. Imagine a world if you're above looking down on it, but you're really below and you should be looking up. It was all very confusing."

"I'll say," said the biggest coyote.

"Shhh!" said the cat.

"Her crew sat, and they deliberated for a long time on what it meant to break through a wall at the bottom of the mountain and stick their heads out into bright sunlight—their heads poking through the blue sky, high, high above the world *below*. No one knew what it meant. They knew it wasn't an illusion, though, because every single one of them had seen it." Bergen fell silent and stared up at the sky for several minutes. The only noise was the train chuffing over the tracks. "I drew a blank," she said finally. "I don't recall the rest."

"Remember, Bergen," said Frederick. "The leader thought to herself: 'We're up here looking down . . . ' "

The words spun around the coal car, zigzagging back over themselves: *downnnnnnn hereeeeeee lookinggggggg uppppppp.*

The coyotes laughed and clapped and shouted, "Again. Do that again!"

The sound slipped like mercury along the rim of the coal car and turned blue as it sped toward Frederick, its voice rising: *upppPPPPPP.* Around his head it spun like a gyroscope before shifting to red and escaping with a bellowed *DOWwnnnnnn* that grew deeper in pitch as it moved away. The sound swung back and forth around the car until Frederick sucked it in. Then he opened his beak wide and an old woman's voice mused as if in thought, "I'm poking my head through the top of somebody's sky!"

"How'd you do that?" asked the cat.

"They don't call me a mockingbird for nothing," said Frederick, and he opened his mouth wide and the woman's voice said. "I've gotta get down there—check this out."

"Why don't we," said a man's voice coming from Bergen's mouth, startling her, but it continued, "tunnel along the curve down to the edge where the sky meets?"

An old woman's laugh broke from between Frederick's beak. "Do you know how many miles that is?" the voice snorted. "No, I'm gonna jump."

"Do you know how far down that is if you jump?" shouted the man through Bergen's mouth. "Miles!"

"So!" said the woman. "I've jumped miles. Find me my big chute. I'll go slow and check it out as I go. And bring me binoculars and food, too. You never know what I'll find down there."

"Hey, wait! Hasn't it occurred to you that you might get down there, but how the hell are you going to get up?"

"That's the kind of thing you might ask a man climbing Everest. Where there's a will, there's a way," she squawked from between Frederick's sharp beak.

"How will you get up?" the man shouted from Bergen's mouth.

"I'll climb."

"Climb what?"

"The rope you'll drop down to me."

"Sure!" he said. "Sure. A seven-mile-long rope."

"Sure," said the woman.

"Where are we going to get such a thing?"

"Isn't this the age of technology? Make one. I'll climb it. Give me some jumars. I'll climb it."

"Superwoman, aren't you."

"Hey, listen kid," she said. "If you can make a rope that long, you sure as hell can pull me up. You make problems where there aren't any. You just have to ask the right questions instead of deciding it's impossible. Nothing's impossible, kid. The mind's the limit."

"A preacher, too! Just what we need, a goddamn preacher. Going to drop on down there and convert the natives? What if the natives aren't friendly? Have you ever thought of that?"

"What people aren't friendly to someone dropping in from the sky?" asked the woman from Frederick's beak.

"So you'll play the divine messenger," boomed Bergen's mouth.

"Sure. And I'll take you with me. You can play the dark force, the power of evil. How do you like that? Where would we be without the doomsayers?"

The voices stopped, and the only sound in the car was the thrumming of the train down the track. The coyotes looked back and forth from Frederick's beak to Bergen's mouth.

"So?" said the biggest.

Frederick shook his head and a song gurgled up from his throat. "I guess they're gone," he said.

"It's coming back to me," said Bergen. "Someone handed the old woman a pair of binoculars, and she saw what looked to be a desert community much like the one above her."

The old woman's voice again mused from Frederick's bill. "Few trees. I don't see any poles that would indicate electric lines, but it's hard to tell from this height. Someone bring me my pack, a reserve. Help me strap it all on. Who packed it?"

"It's yours," said the man's voice from Bergen's mouth. "You did, didn't you?"

"Is this the biggest one you could find?"

"It's the red and white striped one. It's big. They'll see you coming. Are you sure you want to do this?"

"Of course I'm sure," said the woman's voice.

"And she jumped," said Bergen in her own voice.

"Just like I was going out an airplane door," said the woman from Frederick's beak.

"She pulls the cord and the chute pops," said Bergen.

"I pack 'em well," said the woman's thoughts from Frederick's beak.

"She watches it stream and billow over her head, feels the snap as the air pockets under the canopy and pulls her up," said Bergen.

"Woop!" chortled the woman from Frederick's mouth. "And I'm floating downnnnnnn." The word tore loose from his beak and raced past the "upppppppp" that'd just sprung from Bergen's mouth. The colors shifted into white, and then there was silence.

"What in the world's going on here?" bellowed one of Picasso's bulls as it balanced on the cattle car coupled behind the coal car.

"Bergen, you've got a skewed sense of humor," said the cat.

"I didn't create him," said Bergen as the bull pawed and snorted. "Honest!"

"What do we do now?" asked the biggest coyote.

"Invite him to tea," said the cat.

The bull roared, and the train slowed to a stop. Frederick flapped up to the rim opposite the bull. "Oh, oh!" he said. "You haven't seen anything yet!"

Footsteps crunched over the cinder, the sound growing louder until it stopped by the coal car. Slowly, the faces of the ladies of Avignon and the horse from Guernica appeared above the rim.

The coyotes shrieked and hid their heads under their paws.

"What have you done, Bergen?" hiccuped the cat.

"I honestly don't know."

The ladies' faces began to melt into the coal car, hot colors sizzling down the black sides. "Eeck!" cried the cat as it arched its back, fur spritzing like sparklers, its upshot tail poking Bergen in the eye.

"Owwww!" cried Bergen.

"Ha, ha, ha! A little tail for the *vieja verde*," chortled

the bull.

"*El Malo!*" cried Bergen.

"Thought you could get rid of me, did you?" said the bull as it jumped into the coal car. The coyotes tightened their paws over their heads, and the cat hissed. ·

"Where's Katherine?" asked Bergen.

"Here I am," said Katherine's voice from the lump of paint that had formed at the bottom of the coal car.

"What good's she to us like that?" asked Bergen.

The bull licked the spot, and Katherine rose, disheveled, but smiling. "We really fooled you, didn't we!" she said, laughing a big belly laugh.

"I should've known," said Bergen. "I always knew the burrito man was full of bull."

"Ohhhhh!" groaned Frederick, the cat, and the coyotes, who'd finally raised their heads. "Bad joke!"

"What is this? 'Pick on Bergen Klein Day'?" she asked.

"Isn't every day?" asked the bull as he transmogrified into old John.

"I kinda like you the other way," said Katherine, brushing up against him.

"That's sick!" said Bergen.

The train started up again.

"Who's driving this thing?" she asked.

"Aren't you?" asked John.

"Seriously," said Bergen.

"I am serious," he said, his eyes big as needle heads.

"I'll see," said Frederick. He flew off but was back in two heartbeats. "You won't believe this."

"Who?" asked the cat.

"Picasso!"

"Picasso?" asked the cat.

"Dressed like an engineer, but with those striped pants he used to wear."

"You're joking," said Bergen.

"Yup!" said Frederick. "Just some old guy, scratching up under his engineer's cap, saying 'Don't know what come over me.'"

"Well," said the cat. "We've still got a ways to go, right fellas?"

"Right . . . right . . . right," chorused the coyotes.

"So," said the cat, circling a claw in the air, "time for a story!"

"Story, story, story!" shouted the coyotes.

"What's going on here?" asked Katherine as she snuggled next to John at the opposite end of the coal car.

"Bergen was telling us the story about the miner who broke through the roof of the sky."

"Before I was so rudely interrupted," huffed Bergen.

"Just tell the story," said the cat, Frederick, and the coyotes.

"Yeah," said Katherine and John. "Tell the story."

"I don't remember it," said Bergen.

"Story!" shouted everyone.

"If I could, I would."

"Oh, shit!" squawked the old woman's voice from Frederick's beak.

The coyotes laughed and clapped.

"My chute's got a rip, and I'm going down faaaaaasssssttt!"

Air whooshed from Frederick's beak until something thumped in the center of the coal car. The soft feel of chamois fluttered down over Bergen's face.

"What the heck?" said the biggest coyote, digging his way out from under the red and white silk.

"Ohhhh!" moaned a lump under the cloth.

"What's going on here?" asked the cat.

John flipped back the parachute.

"Aaargh!" gurgled Bergen and the lump simultaneously.

"Do you see what I see?" whispered the cat to John.

"*Doppelgänger*," he whispered.

"Double what?" whispered the biggest coyote.

"*Doppelgänger*. But this one's definitely not a shadow."

Bergen and her double just stared. The face each was looking at was her own.

In her double's eyes, Bergen saw the road to her grandma and grandpa's house. The seat she sat on swayed with the motion of the wheels over the deep-rutted ground. "EeeYup!" said the driver, clicking his tongue as he slapped the reins lightly on the backs of two white horses whose shoulders were almost as high as the swaying seat.

"Me," said the little girl sitting next to the driver, her hair swinging back and forth against the sides of her face. "Me. Let me do that."

"No, Miss Bergen. That's nothing for a tiny girl to be doing. Them horses if they get away, why they'll tip this wagon for sure. They's big ones, *ja*?"

"Just for a bit?"

"No, it won't do you no good to use your city ways on me, miss. When a man says no, it's no he means for sure," said the driver as he flipped the reins leaning forward toward the horses. "Look past them trees. See there, your grandpa's house?"

The house stood shining silver in the sun.

"It's very pretty," said Bergen.

"Pretty!" snorted the driver. "Logs, they're not pretty.

That is just the sun's trick to make you think you are coming home to heaven."

Bergen watched the house grow bigger as the horses rocked the wagon down the hill. "Whoaaa!" shouted the driver, pulling back on the reins. "Whoaaa, Belle. Hold up there, Star."

"Dowwwnnnnnnn!" sang the child as the wagon bumped fast after the cantering horses.

"They can smell them oats," said the man. "Whoaaa! Hungry beggars aren't you? Whoaaa!"

"Dowwwnnnnnnn!" called Bergen as they rolled toward her grandparents' house. "Dowwwnnnnnnnnnn!"

"Whoaaa, now, whoaaa. We got to turn this corner at a decent speed," said the man, but the horses raced into the long drive toward the house, tipping the wagon onto the two wheels on Bergen's side, nearly dumping her into the ditch. "Hold on, child. Whoaa!"

Bergen grabbed tight to the back of the seat and to the metal handhold at her side. Her teeth chattered with each fast bump of the wagon, and her eyes bounced fuzzy over the figure running out of the house, toward the wagon.

"Your grandpa," shouted the man to Bergen as he pulled tight on the reins. Olaf ran toward them, his arms upraised and waving. The horses shied, slowed, and trotted, snorting, toward the house.

"Got some runaways there," said Olaf as he swung into the wagon and chucked Bergen under the chin. "You come home to grandpa, Bergie?" His laughing blue eyes caught hers and tugged like a buttonhook at the tip of her spine. She giggled.

"What's my girl laughing about?" he asked as he hugged her to him as the wagon rolled toward the house.

"Your eyes tickle me inside," she said. "All the way down."

Olaf threw back his head and roared with laughter. "Hother, you hear this granddaughter of mine? A splash of aquavit, *ja*?"

"She wanted to drive them horses," said Hother.

"She did, did she?" said Olaf, squeezing Bergen tight. "Just like her grandma, is she?"

"Sure see a touch," said Hother as he pulled the horses right toward the barn, and tugged back hard on the reins. "Hold up, now."

As the horses stopped, Olaf hopped to the ground and reached his arms up to Bergen. She jumped into his hands, and her white skirt belled wide with air and landed in the pupils of the *doppelgänger*'s eyes.

Bergen watched as the light grew up, up, up the stairwell as the little girl climbed barefooted, her white flannel nightgown wrapping around her ankles, a lit matchstick glowing behind her cupped hand.

"Do I have to sleep up here all alone, grandma?"

"You'll not be alone, child. We'll be in this room right next to you. See, look in here."

The match blew out as Nina opened the door. Bergen whimpered.

"Don't cry, honey. Remember what I told you."

Bergen took a matchstick from behind her ear and scratched it up along the door jamb. The sulfur smell burst in her nostrils as the blue flame peeled the dark from Nina's face. "You see," she said, taking Bergen's hand. "With that match behind your ear, you got nothing to fear."

"That's a rhyme," said Bergen. "I know another one: my momma taught me. 'Round and round she goes. Where she falls, nobody knows.' Is this my room?"

"Right here, right next to ours. Careful with the match. Now, see, lift the chimney off the lamp gently like this, set it on the dresser, and put your left fingers here," Nina said as she covered Bergen's fingers with her own. "Now touch the wick with your match—that's right—and turn the knob slowly until the flame's just right. There! Now blow out your match, and put the chimney back on the lamp, and hop into bed."

Bergen shook her match, slid the glass back into the prongs, and jumped, sinking, onto the bed. "It's soft!"

"Feathers," said Nina. "It's a feather bed."

Bergen slid down between the rough, white sheets. "They smell like sunshine," she said.

"*Ja*," said Nina as she turned down the lamp.

Bergen watched the large gold circle on the ceiling get smaller and smaller. "Why does the center get blacker when the light gets smaller?" she asked.

"That's the light's shadow sucking itself in," said Nina, sitting on the edge of the bed. "When you pack it all together like that, it gets very, very, very dark!"

85

"Do you tell stories like my momma?"

"Why sure. Where do you think she got them stories of hers?"

"From you?"

"*Ja.*"

"How'd she get them?"

"What do you mean, honey?"

"How'd they get inside of her voice."

Nina laughed and squeezed her. "I can see you're a looker. That's the best kind of people. Those that watch, listen, and learn."

"Why?"

"Oh! Even better yet. Not just a 'how' girl. She's a 'why' girl. Oh, that's the best. Now you save your curiosity for tomorrow, and then I'll show you a very, very special little thing. Okay?"

"OooooooooKAY!" said Bergen as she raised up to kiss her grandma and then fell back, floating soft into the down.

And in her double's eyes, Bergen saw lace curtains billowing out over the bed and brushing back to the window. Again the wind lifted them, and they floated up, the hem tickling the child's face as they drifted by. Bergen woke and rubbed her nose. Above her the curtain played, and the sun, dusting through it, scattered laced light across the ceiling and on the back of her hands as it rode the wind's breath, tickling past her, sucked back into the open window.

Downstairs the screen door slapped, and footsteps crossed to the bottom of the stairs. "Time to get up, you sleepyhead!" called Nina, her voice circling up the stairs like the lines on a barbershop pole.

"Up! Up! Up!" Bergen sang back, matching her words with the wind pushing the curtain high toward the ceiling. As the curtain fell back toward the window, Bergen bounced to her knees so the lace clung to her. She laughed and stuck her head out the window. The sun slipped soft, gentle as her mother's hands, over her head. Tears filled her eyes and dropped like snowflakes to the grass far below.

"Breakfast," called Nina from the stairwell. "Come and get it."

As Bergen dipped under the curtain, a voice filled her head.

"I love you."

"Momma?" said Bergen as she looked fast around the room.

No one was there.

"Bergen."

She looked through the shadow of lace out toward the pine trees that stood on the North side of the house.

"I love you."

There, sitting high in one of the pines, was an eagle, bright as a $20 gold piece in the morning light.

"Bergen, I love you."

"Momma?"

The eagle cocked its head from side to side.

"You look like a chicken when you do that!" said Bergen, laughing as she fell backward into the down, her white nightgown covering her head.

In the *doppelgänger*'s eyes, Bergen watched as the child and her grandma knelt by a pond, their noses almost touching the surface.

"Do you see it?" whispered Nina, pointing to a little form dancing in the shade.

"No," whispered the child.

"There it is," whispered Nina as the little creature swam into the light.

Bergen slipped her hands into the water and under the shape.

"Cup your hands like this," said Nina. "And bring them up very, very slowly."

Bergen raised her hands and studied their little pool of water. The creature darted back and forth.

"It's looking for the shade," said Nina as she held her hand over Bergen's. "I'll be the tree."

The creature spun in the shadow.

"See life moving through it?" asked Nina.

Bergen watched the heart beating like a whirligig, spinning circles under the translucent skin.

"I want to show grandpa."

"Okay," said Nina. "We'll get him and bring him back here."

"Can't we take her to grandpa to see?"

"I don't know, honey. Creatures don't like to be taken

from their homes."

"I would bring her back," said Bergen staring at the pulsing heart under the silvery skin.

"Well, I guess then it's okay."

"Okay!" said Bergen.

They walked slowly, through the woods, to the edge of the field, the small shape swimming in the pool of Bergen's cupped hands.

"There's grandpa," said Nina.

"Grandpa, grandpa," called Bergen as she ran to where he swung his scythe at the feet of the clover. "Grandpa, look!"

She ran to him, the water spilling.

"What you got there, Bergie?" asked Olaf, looking into her hands.

"A creature! She's alive," said Bergen as she looked down at the small shape drying in the heat of her hand. "Oh, no! Is she going to die?"

"I've got water," said Olaf as he took off toward the trees on the side of the field.

Bergen shadowed the creature with her head, but still the fan heart stopped spinning, and all the black spots under the clear skin stopped pulsing. "Is she dead, grandma?"

"Let's go home, child," said Nina, her soft hands falling like doves on Bergen's tears.

Over the double's eyes puffed a cloud of flour as Nina wumped the dough on the table. The child sat by the closed window, picking the dry bits off the geraniums planted in rusting Prince Edward tins.

"Don't be sad, Bergie," said Olaf, rocking by the table. "All things got to die, but that don't mean they're gone."

"Show her that strip of yours," said Nina as she folded the dough and pressed into it with the heels of her hands.

"Where's the newspaper that come yesterday?"

"But you haven't read that yet," said Nina.

"That don't matter," said Olaf as he cut a two inch-wide strip from the top of his newspaper. He held the ribbon of paper spread at arm's length. "Look, Bergie."

"Now watch grandpa, child," said Nina as she pressed her palms into the dough.

"See, Bergie," he said as he twisted the left end of the strip one turn. "Now you get that glue and rub it right there."

Bergen took the mucilage bottle from the windowsill and dabbed the rubber cap on the left end.

"Good girl!" said Olaf as he pressed the two ends together. "Now we'll let that dry a minute, and then I'll show you the secret."

To the thump of the bread dough on the table, Olaf hummed Grieg's 'In the Hall of the Mountain King,' puffing the notes over the glued spot.

"You got that piece a charcoal, Grandma?" he asked after a bit.

"In the top drawer of the dresser, I believe."

"Here, Bergie. Press your fingers right there," he said handing her the strip. "Like that, *ja*. Hold it tight." He slid across the floor like a skater, humming, and slid into the front room. They heard him rummaging.

"In your drawing box," called Nina.

"Forgot I had a drawing box," mumbled Olaf. They heard the drawer slide closed, and he waltzed back into the room, slipping into the chair next to Bergen. "There. That's dry enough. Now I want you to draw a line right down the middle of this circle. Like this: just hold the charcoal on the paper while I pull the strip through."

Bergen pressed the stick against the newsprint, and Olaf pulled slowly so that a line appeared right down the middle, bumping over the glued spot, and heading back around until the finish met the start and they started round again.

"Round and round you go," said Bergen.

"Right. Round and round we go. See this," he said, laying the strip on the table so it formed a figure eight. "That's the symbol of eternity. Do you know what that means, Bergie?"

She shook her head.

"Forever. Round and round forever. Your little creature lived here," he said, tracing one side of the loop with his finger. "When it died it was here." He pointed to the glued spot. "That's the interstice. And now it's here," he said, circling the other side.

"She might be too young to understand that," said Nina as she put the dough in a washbasin, covered it, and set it in the sun to rise.

"Round and round she goes," sang Bergen, making

figure eights over the strip.

"Maybe not too young," said Olaf. "Here, Bergie, let me show you something else. I'm going to take these scissors and cut along the line you drew. What do you think I'll get?"

"A circle?" asked Bergen.

Olaf snipped away until he came back to the glued spot. Then he gave a shake. "Right! One big circle. How'd you know that?"

"I don't know," said Bergen with a shrug.

"What if I cut it again? Will the circle get bigger?"

"Yes," said Bergen.

Olaf cut through the center of the paper. "One?" he said as he got back to the start.

"One," said Bergen, clapping her hands.

Olaf shook the strip. One circle fell away, caught looped in the other.

"Two!" said Bergen.

"That happens in life sometimes, too. Sometimes when you almost die, your circle splits and a part of you goes into the dreamtime."

"Now she's really too young to understand that," said Nina as she dusted the flour off her hands and lifted Bergen into her lap.

"Round and round we go," said Bergen, taking the strip from Olaf. "Round and round, and where she falls . . . "

A belled skirt swung across the double's eyes.

"Uppppppp!" called the little girl. "Push me higher, grandpa. Higher! Higher! I want to poke a hole in the sky."

"Not too high now," said Nina from her chair in the shade of the house. "That's an old rope, Olaf."

"*Ja, ja*! You women are always worrying."

"Downnnnnnn!" sung Bergen as she whipped toward the ground, her hair shrouding her face, her fingers sliding over the rough hemp rope. Olaf's hand caught her backside. "Uppppppp!" she called as her hair flew back and the sun spun into her eyes and her toes nearly touched the branches of the biggest old pine.

"Downnnnnnnn," she cried as the rope snapped as the smell of sun-hot needles dusted her nostrils as she spun in fast somersaults toward Nina's screaming mouth and the bright silvered wood of the house.

Uummmph.

"So which one of you is the real Bergen?" asked God as he swung the rocking chair across the room, leaving tracks on the freshly waxed hospital floor.

"I am," said Bergen and her double simultaneously from their corners of the couch.

"Which?"

"It is I," they both said, pointing to their chests.

"Suckled at the same mother's breast, no doubt about it," said God as he rocked in front of them, chuckling.

"Would you get rid of her?" they said, each glaring at the other.

"Get rid of you both, you mean?"

"Her!" said each stabbing a finger at the other's shoulder.

"Always happy to oblige. Will the real Bergen Klein please stand up," he said.

They both stood.

"Hmmm," said God, studying them. "Trickier than I thought. A little problem of cosmology here. Got a strip of newspaper?"

"Here's one," they said as they both tried to rip the top off *The New Mexican.*

"Here, I'll do that," said God. "Now we need glue."

"Flour and paste," said both Bergens.

"Naw, we don't got none of that here. I know," said God, rocking to the window. "If we can reach that tree . . . "

"A little pine sap!" they said. "That'll do it."

God snagged a dollop on his ragged nail and wiped it on the left end of the strip.

"Funny, I don't remember that pine there when I came in," said both Bergens, examining the tree.

"It wasn't," said God, tearing the paper slowly down the middle, and down the middle again. "Ta da," he said, shaking the strip so one circle caught in the other. "Now for the moment of truth," he boomed and ripped one of the circles at its interstice.

Nothing happened.

He ripped the second circle.

Nothing happened.

"Didn't think it would work. That's dad's trick, not mine. Let's try this," he said as he snapped his left thumb against his ring finger. Slowly the *doppelgänger* dematerialized and drifted like a crystal cloud sucked into the palm of God's hand.

"Good trick," said Bergen, straightening her skirt over her thighs.

"You ain't seen nothing yet," said God as he pulled aces from his right sleeve with his right hand and fanned them out before her.

"How about making Frederick reappear?"

"What d'ya mean?" asked God.

"She squished the life out of him when she fell."

"You're kidding."

"Wish I were," said Bergen as she walked to the window and looked through the bars at the setting sun. Below in the bushes she could see God's bicycle, but Katherine, John, the cat, and coyotes were nowhere to be seen. "Where have they gotten themselves to now?" she mumbled.

"Oh, they'll turn up when the time's right. They always do," said God, shuffling the cards. "Them coyotes got a knack of being just where I think they oughta be. Besides, this isn't such a bad place really. It's just the people kinda get to you is all. No one knows how to play a good game of poker anymore. They're all into chess, if you can believe that. Never was my game. Too cerebral. Not enough at stake. How can you have any fun if nothing's left to chance?" He slapped the deck on the table between the rocker and the couch. "Wanta cut?"

"I trust you," said Bergen as she sank to the couch next to a huge, worn rose embroidered into the fabric. She traced the stitching.

"There's a story behind that," said God as he dealt the cards. "Five-card draw, by the way."

Bergen sorted her cards: the king, queen, and two of hearts next to the ten and nine of clubs. "I'm beginning to think that's the only constant in life—there's always one more story. I'll take one," she said and threw the deuce away.

God slid the top card off the deck and slowly slipped it

over the table's surface. "You sure you want it?"

"Do I have a choice?"

"Well, now that you mention it, I guess the cards are played," said God.

Bergen tipped the corner of the card. "Do you know what it is?"

"Of course."

"Tell me."

"It won't change anything," said God.

"But it makes the game more fun," said Bergen, tapping the card. "If you know what it is, I can wonder if you put it there."

"Now why would I do that?"

"To add a little spice to the game?"

God smiled and tapped the space between his teeth. "You got me there. Jacka hearts," he said. "And you win. A straight beats me."

Bergen flipped the card. The jack of spades grinned up from the table. "Guess some things you don't control," she said as she slipped the card in the center of the four.

"Wish I could," said God, laying his cards on the table. "Wish I could."

Bergen shuffled the cards. "We should have been playing for money."

"Naw," said God, rocking in the chair, the setting sunlight bouncing in arcs off the black greasepaint under his eyes. "The stakes were already pretty high."

"Another?" asked Bergen.

"There isn't time," said God as rocks hit the window.

He slipped out of the rocking chair and sailed across the floor. "Hail, Hail, the gang's all here."

"It's about time," said Bergen, stuffing the cards into a Bicycle-brand box.

Her shoes squealed as a tall, handsome man dressed elegantly in a dove-gray morning coat with a powder pink boutonniere strolled into the room.

"It's him!" her shoes shouted.

"Him who?" asked Bergen.

"Only the governor of this enchanted land, dear lady," said the gentleman, bowing low.

"No, no!" shouted the shoes. "It's him!"

"Hi, Dad!" said God as he raised the window. "You got the key?"

"Right here." He tossed the brass ring to God.

"Dad?" asked Bergen, studying the man's face.

"Yeah, good ole dad," said God as he unlocked the bars. "Coming?"

"After you," said the governor.

"No, *El Malo*," said Bergen. "After you."

"Ah, *vieja*, catching on in your old age!"

"We can't all keep making the same mistakes forever," she said as God helped her through the window.

God pedaled back over the sand until he spotted the rubber raft bouncing along a silver strip of water between banks overgrown with dusty pink flowering tamarisk. He cupped his hands like a megaphone and called, "There's nothing much ahead except more of the same."

"Okay," shouted Katherine as she turned in the prow and waved. She snuggled back against John's side, ducking the snores that scissored like hornets through the air.

"Music of the spheres," said Bergen, stuffing her thumbs in her ears, pushing her neck back against the warm rubber wall of the stern. "What you see in him, I'll never know."

Katherine ruffled John's thinning hair and kissed his cheek. His snores collapsed into a wheezing sigh. "Some things are meant to be," she said.

"Faddle!" said Bergen.

"Old John's not such a bad dude," said the biggest coyote, stretching in the center of the raft.

"Watch out for your claws on that rubber," said Bergen. "You'll spring a leak."

"That settles it," said the cat from its perch on one of

the center supports. "I'm walking."

"You are not," said Bergen. "Just stay right there."

"I'm not getting wet," said the cat.

"You won't get wet," said Bergen.

"Hey, guys," chortled the biggest coyote. "Puss is afraid of getting wet!"

"Oh, poor puss," chorused the coyotes as the biggest dipped a paw in water.

"Remember the immortal words of Heraclitus," purred the cat.

"Who?" asked the coyotes.

"'Can't stick your paw in the same river twice.'"

"What's that supposed to mean?" asked the biggest, looking from its paw to the water and back again.

"Try it and find out," said the cat as it made a great leap for the bank.

"Grandma, where do you think you're going?"

"I'll see you, Bergen, at home," shouted the cat as it disappeared into the bushes.

"Now look what you've done," said Bergen to the coyotes. "She'll get lost, she'll never make it home, and it's all your fault. You always have to tease her, don't you?"

"For goodness sake, Bergen, what's gotten into you?" asked Katherine. "She's a cat! She can't get lost. She'll make it home long before you do."

"Hmpf!" said Bergen, pressing her head back against the warm rubber, closing her eyes.

They were silent for awhile as the raft floated slowly along the trickle of fall runoff, bumping over rocks, dragging occasionally on the sand. John turned in his sleep, and his snores broke like corralled stallions.

"Oh, not again," said Bergen.

The coyotes covered their ears, and Katherine laughed. "He certainly could wake the dead," she said, nudging him, just as God came bicycling fast over the sand, shouting. "Hear that thunder? Zeus is dumping. Better hold on to your hats folks cuz in a minute you'll be on one fast bronco!"

"What are you talking about?" asked Bergen.

God cupped his left ear and aimed it back the way they'd come. "Listen."

A sound like tanks rolling in the distance beat against Bergen's eardrums, grew into a plane gaining altitude, crescendoed into a freight rushing through a tunnel.

"Earthquake?" shouted Bergen over the roar.

"Worse," shouted God, pointing at a story-high wall of buzzing red mud that moved toward them.

"Holy cow!" said the biggest coyote, shoving his paddle into the water. "Paddle!"

"Paddle!" shouted Bergen and Katherine, scooping the water fast with their paddles.

"Paddle!" chorused the coyotes as they pawed the water on each side of the raft, trying to keep ahead of the roiling water descending upon them.

"Faster, faster," puffed God as he pedaled ahead along the beach, looking back so that he didn't see the tree stretched across the bank to the water's edge.

"Watch out, son," shouted John, who'd finally woken,

but it was too late. The last thing they saw as the raft shot past was God, face first in the sand, his bike with bent front tire over him, and the wave pressing hard on top.

They stopped paddling for a moment, looking back, shouting, "Watch out . . . hurry . . . get up . . . run," but the wave swallowed God and moved on toward them like a dinosaur, scooping the raft up its long neck to its back. The neck stretched and the raft shot forward like a roller coaster car, sending them sailing past cottonwoods that fell in the water behind them, yanked out by the roots.

The water finally slowed, slipping under them like silk, and they floated along.

"Can you see him," they whispered to each other, looking up and down river.

"There's his bike," said John, pointing to the silver tangled in the roots of a cottonwood.

They tried to paddle over to it, but the current was too strong and swept them right past.

"He can't be gone," said John, tears in his eyes. "I couldn't manage without him."

"We'll find him," said Katherine just as God's voice popped up above the water.

"Did you hear that?" said Bergen.

The voice shot up again.

"Where is he . . . where . . . do you see . . . ?" they all shouted.

"Hole," shouted God.

"Whole? . . . What does he mean? . . . Whole?"

"Hole! Big hole," shouted God.

"Hole! . . . Oh, hole!"

They looked, but none could see a hole.

"Do you suppose he means that spot up there that's burbling?" asked Katherine as they felt themselves being sucked toward it.

God's voice was louder: "Hole! Watch out! Hole!"

"Oh, shoot," said the coyotes in unison. "Paddle."

They all paddled as hard as they could, trying to shift the raft from its course, away from the foaming water, but it was too late. The raft hit the whitewater head on, rose straight up on its tail, and hung suspended as Bergen somersaulted backwards into the whirlpool.

The torrent closed over her, dark and cold, pounding her down, down, down. She stretched out her arms and swam as hard and fast and strong as she'd ever swum, but the water piled on top of her, colder and darker with a force that spun her round and round. She pulled harder still until her lungs, crackling like paper burning, fought her mouth to open wide, gulp, open wide.

"Mama!"

Joey appeared before her, his face laughing, his arms held wide.

"Mama!"

She circled him in her arms.

"Let go," said a voice in her head. "Let go!"

Bergen held tighter, kicking, trying to surface with Joey.

She felt arms around her, and her head filled with the

image of herself popping like a cork to the surface, buoyed up by a life jacket.

"Just let go!"

Bergen quit struggling.

Up she shot, holding Joey tight.

"You're okay," said God, sputtering, his arms a tight circle around her.

"Joey!" cried Bergen, looking frantically around her.

"It's okay. I got you," said God. "Relax now. Point your toes downstream."

"Joey!" wailed Bergen, beating at God. "Where's Joey? Joey!"

"Downstream, point!" said God, steering her in the icy water.

"Joey," cried Bergen, collapsing against God's arms.

"Shhh," he said, steering her around. "Just float now."

"There they are," shouted the coyotes, backpaddling to keep the raft in place, as God and Bergen floated toward them.

"Grab her," said God, catching hold of the rope on the edge of the raft, hoisting Bergen up.

John and Katherine dragged her into the water-filled raft and propped her against the edge, rubbing her icy hands and feet. The coyotes huffed on her shoes.

"Aaah, aaah," gagged the left shoe. "Bad breath."

"Shut up," sighed the right. "So warm, don't stop."

God pulled himself over the side. "We thought we'd lost you for sure," he said, leaning over her, his dreadlocks dripping in her face.

"Joey," whimpered Bergen. "Joey."

"What's this?" asked Katherine.

"She thought she saw Joey, I guess," said God.

"I did. He was there. Joey!"

"Shh, honey," said Katherine, stroking her hair, rocking her. "You were just imagining things."

"I wasn't. He was there, Katherine. I held him in my arms! Joey!"

God took Bergen's hand in both of his own.

"You!" she said, pulling her hand back. "Why didn't you leave me alone? Leave me to die?"

Tears slipped from God's eyes.

"And where'd I get this damn jacket?" she asked, pulling at the orange fabric that covered her chest.

"Jacket?" asked John.

Bergen looked into his eyes and saw him tucking her into the vest. "You? Why would you . . . "

"The great escape?"

"You!" she screeched, pulling the life jacket off and throwing it at John's feet. "Once again I lose my son because of you!"

"That wasn't my fault," said John.

"No! Not your fault! Go to China, you said. There's a revolution there. We're needed, you said. Not your fault, no!" screamed Bergen.

"You didn't have to go."

"My husband was going because of you; how could I say no?"

"You made your choice."

"You made it for me."

"That's an old grudge, *vieja*. Why not let sleeping dogs lie?"

"Sleeping dogs?"

"Wet dogs, wet dogs," gurgled Bergen's shoes.

"Sure ain't getting any drier," said the biggest coyote, shivering.

"We better bail, folks," said God, wiping away his tears and scooping a bucketful over the side.

"So you finally made it home," said the cat, rising from a patch of sunlight on the window sill, stretching.

Bergen, God, John, and Katherine collapsed into chairs around the kitchen table. The coyotes sprawled on the floor.

"Where's Kristian?" asked Bergen, eyeing the coffeepot perking on the stove.

"I'm not sure you want to know," said the cat.

"He's mad?"

"Worse! He's a nervous wreck—been up, each night, every night, to hear him mumble. Can't sleep; he's so worried about you."

Bergen rocked, crossing her belly with her left forearm, her right index finger crooked, pressing against in her mouth. She shook her head and said, "I wish he wouldn't take his knight errant role so seriously."

John snorted a rusty laugh. "Remember China?"

"Not if I can help it," said Bergen, closing her eyes.

"The wall?"

They tiptoed along the wall, the three of them, silent in the dark shadow that fell over the moon-lipped top. The night ate them with its stillness, the quiet closing like a spinning top into a buzz that sent their eyes searching the dark for its source. They crouched, watching, moving like jackals toward a scent, alone, the three of them, through the night.

Just before morning, they saw the fires down in the valley, across the empty hills, no trees for cover. John pointed up the wall, and they climbed, fingers grabbing night-cold stone, toes tearing chips of rock free, scattering them like mice rattling against rice paper walls. Bergen reached the top first, her fingers groping for a stone to lever her body up, over the edge, when a hand seized her wrist and jerked her like a marionette to the top of the wall. The smell of pickled cabbage pressed against her as the hand grabbed her hair under her cap and yanked her up to a face as puffed as Shiva's. Bergen punched out with her thumbs, pressing against the huge windpipe, kicked out with her heavy boots toward a cloth-padded groin. The hand jerked her out and away so she swung, her hair ripping from its hold, the pain searing her nerves into a tight-held scream that she swallowed as a force hit her captor's body, knocking them both to the rocks. Bergen rolled away and jumped to her feet. There as the sun rose, Kristian slammed the man's head over and over and over against the stone, spilling the pink of brain and blood over the sun-flecked stone, humming a silent fury as he did so.

The man's hands fell, and John and Bergen pulled Kristian's shoulders, looking over their own, pulling him toward the other side of the wall. They slipped down, over the slick stone, into the shadow cast by the sunrise against the wall, onto the tight crunch of ground. Kristian arms encircled Bergen, his tears slipped over her face, down her black sweater, slipping between her breasts like a tongue.

"You're safe!" said Kristian, dropping his armful of white-painted crosses by the stove, slipping into a chair next to Bergen. "I was so worried about you. Where were you?"

Bergen patted his hand. "You worry too much, and I left you a note!"

"'Back soon' was all it said. 'Back soon.' When's 'soon,' Bergie?"

"You might not want to get into it now," said God, lifting the coffeepot from the stove, pouring cups all around. "She's had a bit of a tough time, you know."

"What do you expect?" asked Kristian, pushing his cup aside. "Going off on a wild goose chase like that. I swear, Bergie, sometimes I think you've wasted your whole life chasing your shadow."

God looked at Katherine, John looked at Bergen, the cat looked at the coyotes, and they all howled with laughter.

"What's so funny?" asked Kristian.

"Sh . . . sh . . . sh . . . adow!" sputtered Bergen.

"Shadow? What's so funny about shadows?"

Bergen wrapped her arms around her middle, John beat the table, Katherine wheezed, and God, the coyotes, and cat chorused, "Shadow!"

"Will you kindly let me in on the joke?" asked Kristian.

"Not now," gasped Bergen, wiping tears away.

"I'll tell you later," said John. "Over a beer. At the bar?"

"You buying?"

"Cheap as they come, aren't you?" said John, slugging Kristian's shoulder. "No, *hermano*, when I tell you my news, you'll buy."

"What news?"

"*Con pacencia se gana el cielo*," said John, hugging Katherine.

"Can't anyone around here speak English?" asked Kristian as he jumped from his chair, bounded across the creaking floorboards, and scooped up his crosses. "I have work to do."

"Oh, how's the graveyard coming, Kristian?" asked Bergen.

"Cemetery! And it's nearly clean as a whistle, almost ready for All Soul's, no thanks to any of you."

"Now don't get huffy, Kristian. We're back. What can we do?"

"No," said John, getting up from the table. "You rest. You've got some work ahead of you."

"Yeah," said God, standing. "I think we should all get out of here for awhile—give you some time alone. Okay, gang?"

"Yeah," said the cat and coyotes.

"I'll be back before dark," said Katherine, leaning over and kissing Bergen's cheek.

"Something fishy's going on here," said Bergen as she

watched them walk out the door. She drummed her fingers on the table, sipped her cold coffee, brushed away some crumbs, and pushed back her chair. "Guess I'll paint."

She floated into her studio and examined the canvas on her easel. The undercoating glowed with a life of its own in the evening sun. "This'll do," she said, squeezing mounds of fresh paint onto a clean palette sheet.

She pulled her finest sable brush from the mayonnaise jar at her feet, licked the bristles into a point, dipped them into the white. The brush slid from her hand like a Ouija planchette and landed in the black. She pulled the brush from the mound of paint, but the sable jumped from her grasp and wrote in a calligrapher's hand on the canvas, "Shades of Gray."

"Very funny," said Bergen as the brush danced before her, "but I'm painting crosses." She snatched the brush out of the air, plunged it into a jar filled with water, and stirred vigorously. Bubbles rose to the surface and the word "gray" broke from each. Bergen pulled the brush from the jar and wiped it in a fencing motion on her skirt to remove the water.

"Gray, hunh?"

Her other brushes shot from the old mayonnaise jar at her feet, landed in the blobs on her palette, and flitted to the canvas.

"Whose painting is this anyway?" asked Bergen, trying to pick the brushes out of the air and deposit them in the water jar. As she pulled one down, another escaped, shaking its wet bristles, dabbing more paint, scrubbing it against the canvas as though they were cleaning a window to uncover a view.

"Watch out: you'll wear yourselves out, and I can't afford to replace you," cried Bergen, trying to stop them, sinking finally onto her footstool with a huff. "No control over anything anymore! Even my paintbrushes have a mind of their own."

The picture appeared quickly: a smiling face framed by a spray of red hair bursting from under a white cloche; black hair parted in the middle, slicked behind ears, black staring eyes, a possessive hand; a white gown, short hem dropping into points, white shoes and stockings, lace draping full breasts; a wool coat, black, black coat, black tie, black slacks.

"Looks like my mother," murmured Bergen. "And my father? No, that's not my father."

The brushes whirled and another face emerged between the first two—giant, gloating. Diamond-studded hands pushing, pushing, pushing until tears ran from the other man's eyes over the coat, the tie, the slacks, running into a black river down over his feet.

The woman's painted hand disappeared into the massive red hand of the other. The black-eyed man turned into the background, pulling the river of tears around him like a cloak, his eyes catching Bergen's as he whirled.

"John?" asked Bergen, leaning toward the canvas.

The figure bowed low and was gone.

"This is crazy," said Bergen to the brushes. "You're trying to tell me that love did this to him, made *El Malo* what he is? That *he* loved my mother, but she married my father?"

"Shades of gray," said the sable. "But there's more. Sit back and watch."

Bergen slouched on the footstool, her right hand on her knee, propping her chin with her hand. The brushes whirled the paint into an image of a woman's body hanging limp in a tree, a parachute tangling the trunk.

"I don't want to see that again—please," said Bergen, spinning on the footstool to face the window. "Once in a lifetime is enough. Plenty, in fact."

"It was really a very good day for her to die," said the sable.

"Same day as my mother."

"*Was* it?"

The brush's tone caused Bergen to turn. On the canvas an image of Katherine appeared.

"A body only Rubens could love," sighed the sable.

"*El Malo* seems to have no problem," said Bergen as the brushes whipped the morning-suited John onto the canvas, his arms squeezing Katherine through mounds and mounds of tulle, satin and lace. "What's this? A wedding dress I see?"

"Here comes the bride," sang the brushes as they dropped one by one into the mayonnaise jar.

"You've got to be kidding! She's not going to marry him?"

114

The sable brightened John's smile and lit his eyes with two small dots of white. "Finally, *chica*," said the figure, turning to the image of Katherine. "I've waited nearly a century for you!"

"A century?" asked Bergen.

"*Más o menos, vieja*. What does it matter? Course if you had your way, I know, you'd keep your *mamacita* all to yourself. But, don't you know, there's more than enough to go around," he said, hugging Katherine's great waist.

"*Mamacita*?" asked Bergen, bull-dogging her head toward the canvas. "Mother?"

Katherine turned to Bergen and winked.

Bergen sat on a freshly painted crypt, tracing the rose shadows of the sunset on the blue concrete slab. "It's not that I'm afraid to die, really," she said to Kristian.

"No, you've never been that," he said as he bent to place the last candles in paper bags around the graves. "May I borrow your match?"

She pulled the kitchen match from behind her ear and looked at it. "That's not true," she said as she walked over to where Kristian knelt beside a grave. "I've been plenty scared in my time. Ask Katherine. She knows."

Kristian took the match, struck it on one of the white-painted stones that he'd placed around the graves, and lit a taper. "I sure haven't seen it. In fact, sometimes I could swear you've got a death wish," he said as he moved from wick to wick, until all the bags glowed golden in the night.

"You've done a nice job," said Bergen, looking around her.

Kristian shielded the flame with his hand and the light glinted off the gold that edged his teeth. "Getting a little windy, there, eh, Bergie?"

"Now, Kristian, don't be mean. You act like it's the first time I've complimented you."

"Isn't it?" he asked, hugging her.

"No," she said, running her hand over his loins. "I think there was a time in '42, wasn't there?"

"What a memory you have," he said, tripping his fingers over her lips and chin to her breastbone, his eyes locking with hers. "Lady L."

"Lewd?"

"Lascivious."

"Lecherous."

"Licentious."

"Oh come," said Bergen. "That's going too far!"

"My favorite, then: lickerous," he said, licking her chin.

"You haven't changed a bit," said Bergen, running her fingers through the hair in his ears. "Except gotten furrier."

"Lusty!"

"I'm going to miss you," said Bergen, laying her head on his shoulder.

"Lugubrious, too, I see," said Kristian as he shielded the taper. "The wind's picking up."

John appeared from the dark carrying a large, white-painted cross. "Where do you want it?" he asked.

Kristian pointed the cupped light. "Up on top of the hill, there's a hole I dug."

Bergen watched John trudge up the hill, the wind whirling around his back.

"Now, where were we?" asked Kristian as he bent to relight a candle.

"Love," said Bergen as the wind whistled between

them. "Have I ever thanked you for being you, Kristian?"

He looked over his shoulder, the light slicing across the folds of his cheek. "Bergie! You act as if you really are going to die soon."

"I am."

"Bergie, don't talk like that. I mean, I know when the time comes we've all got to go, but this isn't your time. I'd know it if it were."

"It is, Kristian."

"No," he said, grabbing her hand. "I won't let you go."

"I don't think you have a choice in this, Kristian."

"But I'd be lost without you," he said, falling to his knees, wrapping his arms around her legs.

"Kristian, stand up! You're embarrassing me. John will see."

"I don't care who sees. I won't let you go."

"Ah, there you are," said Katherine, appearing between the rows, her wedding dress swinging against the tombstones as she walked. "Why are you on your knees, Kristian? Proposing to my daughter?"

"Daughter?" asked Kristian, getting slowly to his feet. Light from the crescent moon seeped over the mesa, turning his tears to silver.

"Hey!" called God as he vaulted over the tombstones, followed by the cat and coyotes. "You seen the old man? It's almost time for his wedding."

John's laughter skittered down the hill, and he came rolling after, landing like a stone at God's feet. "Son," he said, dusting himself off. "I better run and change."

"Hurry," called Katherine as John's smile disappeared in the moonlight. "Oh, I can hardly wait. Whata man, whata man, whata man!"

The coyotes set up a howl, the cat scratched its claws against a stone, and Katherine whirled in the moonlight until iridescence slipped over her like silk.

Kristian and Bergen stood with their arms around the other, her head on his shoulder, his head resting against her pure white hair.

"C'mon," called Katherine, clapping her hands. "No one can be sad tonight. It's my wedding night. Dance!" She picked up a scythe leaning against a crypt and hopped it as she spun it under her feet. "Kristian's turn," she said without missing a beat.

"No," he said. "Not me!"

"I'll do it," said God, prizing the spinning blade from Katherine's gyrations. Without missing a turn, he squatted and whirled the blade under his kicking feet.

"Brava!" shouted the coyotes.

"Your turn, Kristian," puffed God, letting the blade spin to a stop.

"Go ahead," said Bergen, pushing him forward. "I've heard stories about you in Russia."

"Rumors, you mean," said Kristian. "And that was how many years ago? When we'd won the war."

"Won the war," said Bergen.

"Won," said Joey, hooting like a red Indian, his hand beating against his little mouth.

"Uncle's coming home!" cried Bergen, lifting him into

her arms and dancing him around the room to the windows.

"Hoohoohoommme," sang Joey from under his patting hand.

"Home!" said Bergen, smiling, looking out over the wine-dark surface of the sea.

"I remember that," said God, dancing Bergen around the graveyard, beating his hand against his mouth. "Hoohoohoommme!"

"You remember that?" asked Bergen, stopping between the tombstones. "How can you remember that?"

John emerged from the dark. "Ah, *vieja verde*, you finally found them bones you was looking for?"

"What bones?" asked Bergen.

"Your son," said John, pointing at God.

"Joey?" She tilted her head back to look at God.

"Sure, *vieja*. You think it was me brought you home?"

"Hoohoohoooommmmmme," sang God, dancing her around the graveyard.

"Joey?"

He laughed and danced her faster around the faces of the others around pulling away moving back fast like whirlpool shadows caught and the moonlight spun circling a cocoon of dark around her laughing faster and faster falling.

Falling.

"Hooooooommmmmmme"

Falling, falling, falling through the slow sibilance toward the light falling.

"Hooooooommmmmmme"

Hands on her, huge hands, slick body slipping under giant hands. "What?" she cried.

"It's twins," were the last words she heard.